Joyce Carol Oates

THE RISE OF LIFE ON EARTH

A New Directions Book

A number of quotations have been taken, in slightly modified form, from *The Nurse's Aide Handbook* by Carmen Carrión Sánchez (New York: Arco Publishing, 1984).

Book design by Sylvia Frezzolini
Manufactured in the United States of America
New Directions books are printed on acid-free paper.
First published clothbound by New Directions in 1991 and as New Directions Paperbook 746 in 1992
Published simultaneously in Canada by Penguin Books Canada Limited

Library of Congress Cataloging-in-Publication Data
Oates, Joyce Carol, 1938–
The rise of life on earth / Joyce Carol Oates.
p.   cm.
ISBN 0–8112–1213–0 (pbk.)
I. Title.
[PS3565.A8R5   1991b]
813'.54—dc20   92–15118
                        CIP

New Directions Books are published for James Laughlin
by New Directions Publishing Corporation,
80 Eighth Avenue, New York 10011

FOURTH PRINTING

FOR THE KATHLEENS.

The picture must give out light on its own,
bodies have their own light that they exhaust
in living. They burn away, they are unlighted.

Egon Schiele in a letter, 1912

PART *One*

One

People made false estimates of her, how was she to blame. Rarely did she lie. She was too proud to lie. Nor even to compose her face in an artful manner to deceive.

For instance: when she was first admitted to Children's Hospital the nurses marveled that she was only eleven years old. In her hearing one of them exclaimed, "Oh I can't believe it—*her?*—*that one?*"

Kathleen Hennessy with her pie-shaped face, pie-shaped maturing breasts, her pale, plump, soft, seemingly textureless flesh like that of a mollusk pried from its shell . . . and her recessed eyes that were darkly bright and alert, though betraying no expression; her delicate complexion riddled with tiny pimples like buckshot. There was something unsettlingly adult in her stoic resistance to pain and such extremes of discomfort and physical humiliation she was obliged to bear at the hands of the hospital staff, and something precocious about her small, pert, moist, pink rosebud of a mouth, a miniature mouth, that reminded observers of a part of the female anatomy that is private and should not be exposed to casual eyes.

Her hair was gone as if it had never been. Frizzed matted hair of the hue of woodshavings and with that degree of languid curl. They'd had to cut it off in clumps, in the emergency room, then shave her skull, to treat her for head injuries. They'd perhaps have shaved her hair off in any case to rid her of lice.

When near the end of Kathleen's hospitalization she began to smile at certain of the nurses, the nice nurses, the ones who were kind to her, it was remarked how her entire face and even, in a way, her quivering-soft body seemed to shift with an expression of . . . radiant hope. Yes: something like that. But of course Kathleen Hennessy did not smile often.

Kathleen had been brought by ambulance to

Children's Hospital, Detroit, Michigan, early in the morning of April 6, 1961, with a head concussion, broken ribs, a broken finger, a blackened eye, and numerous bleeding wounds and bruises on her head and face, torso, legs from a severe beating her drunken father had given her after the disappearance of her mother from the family's current place of residence in the Motor City Inn on lower Dequindre Street. Mr. Hennessy had beaten both Kathleen and her six-year-old sister Nola in what was described as a "rampage"; Nola never regained consciousness, dying in the ambulance en route to the hospital. That her little sister had *died,* was thus *dead,* that Mr. Hennessy had been arrested and locked away in a maximum security detention center, charged with murder, aggravated assault, and resisting arrest, no one explicitly informed Kathleen yet even in her entranced, blank-eyed state she seemed to know these facts. And the fact too, as it would be borne out by Time, that her mother would never reappear to claim her.

Yet the miracle was, a small miracle it was but remarked upon, how, by degrees, slowly at first then with visible acceleration, this battered child came to bloom in Children's Hospital, even in the crowded public-welfare ward of sixteen beds and continuous commotion. Even in the face of her injuries, the insult of the shaved head and nowhere to hide: very like one of those plumped-out hydrangea blossoms on the potted plants the nurses sometimes brought her, not gifts exactly, but borne with the smiles of gift-giving, plunder of an innocent sort retrieved from the rooms of patients who had died—for it was a fact of life in Children's Hospital that family members, stricken with grief and numbed with shock, had little interest in taking home the melancholy accumulations of flowers, candy, stuffed toys, books, and the like brought to such patients. "Here, Kathleen—something nice for *you*," the nurses would call out, "—just for *you*." For Kathleen Hennessy had no visitors except now and then someone from the social-welfare agency, thus no gifts. Yet she was so uncomplaining: so docile, so seemingly sweet-natured. If only all their patients were like Kathleen Hennessy!— so the nurses concurred. Repeated blood samples, two spinal taps, brain scans, IV fluids dripping into her veins, even for a time a catheter—Kathleen bore such procedures with an adult fortitude that few adults in fact possess: for even the most excruciating pain, from the spinal tap needle for instance, evoked in her a palpable resistance to the expression of pain, not screams and struggle but subterranean shudders pulsing through her, a slick clammy sweat breaking on her body, her eyes rolling up in her head as *"Oh—"* she whispered, the very expulsion of sound muffled, muted, apologetic, "—oh oh *oh*—" It was as if whatever her father had done to her had left the girl so permanently entranced, little else might draw out her fullest response.

Certain of the nurses vied with one another in their little acts of kindness to her. A nurse named Betty Lou and a nurse named Hazel, both older women, mothers, their children long grown and departed. They loved to make Kathleen Hennessy smile—that sudden startled almost-pretty smile roused out of the rather slack, sallow face. That faint embarrassed murmur, ". . . oh thank you," barely audible, out of the miniature mouth. But you could see in her eyes how much it meant to her: a purloined box of chocolates, a stuffed panda with a synthetic glare to its fur, unused coloring books, a pot of hydrangeas with big blue blossoms that looked dyed but were genuine.

Much of the time, however, Kathleen Hennessy was wordless and preoccupied; perhaps not preoccupied but dreamy, inert, blank, her left thumb loosely stuck in the corner of her mouth, damp with spittle. She was not waiting for anyone to come to claim her, she showed no sign of wishing to leave the hospital or of anticipating her discharge. Now the staff knew she was only eleven years old and not fifteen or sixteen they attributed her passivity to her age. She ignored or did not in fact hear conversations at other beds in her ward; rarely did she acknowledge remarks made to her except by nurses, interns, residents she'd come to know. In the day room she did not watch television so much as gaze toward it, her eyes' surface attracted by that motile surface, otherwise unengaged. Regaining her strength, by visible degrees, she began to eat with more appetite, her jaws slowly grinding, insect duty and rapacity it sometimes seemed, her small dark recessed eyes gleaming and her entire body involved in the act of swallowing so Betty Lou or Hazel might be moved to say, "—That's a good girl, Kathleen," stooping over her, smiling, motherly, "—what a *good girl.*"

It was known on the ward that Kathleen Hennessy's father had beaten her and that he had killed her younger sister. It was not known why.

The whereabouts of Kathleen's mother, or if in fact there was a mother—no one quite knew.

The nurses were incensed: "Isn't she sad!—tragic!—do you suppose she'll ever talk?"

And: "Isn't she brave—do you suppose she remembers?"

And, most vehemently: "God love her, what a *saint!* So *young!*"

At the end of her twenty-six-day stay in Children's Hospital Kathleen was to be discharged to Wayne County Children's Welfare Center, no mother having turned up, no relatives, and Mr. Hennessy in jail unable to post bond, and as she was preparing to leave her nurse friends hugged her goodbye one by one, and she made an effort to hug them in return, clumsily, shyly, not accustomed to such extravagances of affection, her face flushed and her eyes damp with tears, there was Hazel so yeasty-smelling giving her a wet kiss on the cheek, there was Betty Lou, stocky, big-breasted, an older image of Kathleen Hennessy herself, Betty Lou with the light eyes in the red-ruddy face was one who had often brought Kathleen any number of surprises and treats and now at their farewell this woman pressed into Kathleen's hand a mysterious object the girl took at first to be a necklace of crystal beads, or were they actual jewels: their octahedron shapes, their precisely cut glittering facets, so lovely and so unexpected! And there was a tiny silvery cross at one end with a tiny silvery figure meant to be a man's, near-naked, the man's arms and legs outstretched so Kathleen stared and stared and Betty Lou whose scent was of germicide-detergent solution and talcum powder hugged Kathleen with especial vehemence and said, fierce in her ear, "This is a rosary, Kathleen—you'll find out what it's for."

Two

In July 1961 in the heat of midsummer in Detroit, Joseph Hennessy, forty-two years old, unemployed, formerly a metalworker, no prior police record though well known to the county welfare agency as a "difficult" client, was brought before a district judge to be tried on charges of second-degree murder, aggravated assault, and resisting arrest—having waived his constitutional right to a trial by his peers but having refused to enter a plea of guilty to a reduced charge of manslaughter as his lawyer strongly advised.

Why plead guilty to any charges when he was innocent?—thus Hennessy cagily shook his head, grim, grinning, expelling a harsh mirthless noise like escaping steam meant to be laughter of a knowing ironic kind. Saying, "Not me. Son of a bitch, not *me*."

It was Joseph Hennessy's story that he had never beaten either of his daughters though in his general attitude he seemed to acknowledge that one, or both, might be dead. It was as if they had ceased to exist, thus could have no specific connection with him, thus he was innocent of all charges muttering and laughing "Son of a bitch, son of a bitch." He could give no coherent account of what had occurred between approximately midnight and four o'clock of the morning of April 6, 1961, in the single-room motel unit of the Motor City Inn in which he and his family had been living since midwinter. He spoke frequently and excitedly of his wife whom he blamed for his arrest—for "causing trouble." He seemed to think that she had telephoned the police and had testified against him at police headquarters; that she was somewhere close by the courtroom, perhaps listening in. He was a fattish muscular bullet-headed man of five feet six inches, one hundred ninety pounds, with thinning colorless hair like bleached grass, an alcoholic's broken and pitted skin, a small fleshy-pink mouth with a habit of sucking itself inward after he spoke, as if in retraction of his words. His head appeared to have no chin and his thick neck disappeared into his upper back with the impermeability of a tree trunk. The young man from the State of Michigan Department of Public Advocacy who was his lawyer, the young man from the Wayne County District Attorney's Office who was his prosecutor, even the massive burly armed police guards who oversaw his behavior in the airless little courtroom on the fourth floor of the City–County Building on Woodward Avenue were instinctively wary of him, physically alert. Though taciturn, virtually mute during most of the proceedings, Hennessy gave an impression of matter precariously poised, or balanced; a landslide about to discharge itself down a mountain, a tense gathering of molecules about to strike in a single improvised yet lethal direction. He grinned often, muttering behind his hand, and emitted that sound as of escaping steam.

Then during the testimony of a man identified as the manager of the Motor City Inn Hennessy got to his feet and began shouting, throwing his arms about, his face contorted in fury and in that instant beet-red, and within seconds the guards arm-wrestled him to the floor then hauled him skillfully and even gracefully back up into his chair, the entire procedure requiring a briefer space of time nearly than one would require to observe it let alone absorb it: and now at last this electric discharge of energy had occurred, now the guards and the bull-necked defendant had established their relationship exclusive of though contingent upon their relationship with the other men in the courtroom, the men wearing suits, neckties, long-sleeved shirts to establish the propriety of cuffs at their wrists, those men with a look about their faces of groomed and determined civilization; that fearfulness in their eyes no degree of authority could entirely assuage, now this establishment of boundaries had been asserted, Joseph Hennessy sat hunched and sullenly respectful in the airless room refraining almost disdainfully from interrupting as one by one the prosecution's several witnesses came forward into the purview of the plump youngish bespectacled judge and were identified and duly sworn in and gave their accounts of what they insisted had occurred in the Hennessy's motel unit, what they had seen with their own eyes or had heard or were led to infer, and the red second hand moved in its circumscribed space in an antiquated-looking clock high on the rear wall above the door, and the limp yet still gaudily resplendent flag of the United States of America drew the eye at the front of the room, and sunshine rendered gauzy and affable by pollutants in the urban air shone beyond the broad antiquated windows overlooking a foreshortened block of Woodward Avenue going south to the river. What had these words, these testimonies, to do with a man's raging fists, a man's booted feet kicking soft flesh!—how feeble, set beside the fury of a chair leg wielded in a man's able fist! Hennessy hunched his bullish shoulders, screwed up his face in an expression of contempt. *You can't catch me,* he seemed to be saying, challenging—*you don't even know my true name.*

Yet the men in charge, the men in suits, ties, clean smart summer shirts, continued their agenda. It was their agenda—this was how they made their livings. Except for the prosecution's trump card, the taped testimony of Kathleen Hennessy, and a three-way discussion among the judge, the prosecutor, and the defense attorney as to the admissibility of this evidence, the trial of Joseph Hennessy seemed a matter of bookkeeping, of legal documentation and procedures mechanical and ineluctable as the movement of the clock; Hennessy was out of it, disdainfully. He snuffled, he cleared his throat loudly and disgorged clots of phlegm into an already filthy Kleenex. The young judge took off his glasses and briskly cleaned the lenses and replaced them, regarding Joseph Hennessy through a filter of discreet repugnance as a prudent man might regard a solar eclipse through a piece of smoked glass . . . for here was a man who had not only savagely beaten his two young daughters in a drunken rage, killing one of them with repeated blows to the head, but who betrayed not the slightest remorse for his act; beyond that and in its way more astonishing than that he betrayed not the slightest awareness of the novelty of this absence of remorse, nor could he gauge its effect upon those who were negotiating his legal fate—how many years he would spend in the Michigan prison system. He shifted in his seat as if his trousers fit him too tightly, he spat a large glistening clot of phlegm into a tissue, how bored he was, how uninvolved.

And then the forty-five-minute taped testimony of Kathleen Hennessy was played, over the defense lawyer's objection.

And then Joseph Hennessy seemed to rouse himself, to actually listen: sitting suddenly stiff, attentive: his head back-tilted at an uncomfortable angle and his eyes starkly open, fixed on a high corner of the room. Kathleen Hennessy the "surviving" daughter was only eleven years old thus could not be subjected to courtroom testimony and cross-examination, and now her taped voice was made to ring out unnaturally loud with an authority none of the previous voices had possessed. She spoke slowly, gropingly, with an air of wonder, her words seemingly disconnected as the actions of a sleepwalker, slow flat vague words, uttered with effort, the pauses between the words sibilant as if with unarticulated speech, the interstices of the words charged as if with static electricity:

> . . . Daddy . . . hit me.   I don't . . . know
why.   I . . . don't know if   I was bad.
  He . . . hit me and,   and Nola . . .
    We were in bed and he,   woke me up, he . . .
hit me . . . he was hitting and . . .   He . . . asked where
    Mommy was but I . . .   Nola was scared, she . . . was
  crying,   I tried to crawl under the bed but . . .
    Daddy had a stick in his hand . . . I was bad I guess
          and Nola, she . . .   I couldn't . . .
    I don't know why he hit us, I . . . don't know   why
            I . . . was crying.

And so for forty-five minutes in the silent courtroom as everyone, nearly all men, listened intently, as much to the awkward pauses between the words as to the words themselves, to that bodiless child's voice profound because bodiless, that slow flat dull dazed hypnotized voice beyond any apparent capacity for subterfuge as it was beyond any apparent human volition, and when the tape ended Hennessy's lawyer conferred with him, the defendant now grimly shaken, face the color of wet newsprint, mouth sucked into the pinched little orifice beneath his broken-veined nose and his small furtive eyes darting about from face to face seeking to know how bad it was, how bad it really was, how badly he was being judged by these men in charge of running civilization, and lawyer and client hastily conferring together decided to plead guilty after all if the bargain could still be struck: Hennessy would agree to second-degree manslaughter and the other charges if they might be similarly reduced to wind things up this very morning and clear the court for the next case.

And so it was.

Three

. . . the children's shelter behind the high
chainlink fence on Hogan Street, then the Chesneys' asphalt-sided house on Eleventh Street, the
first of several homes in which Kathleen Hennessy
would be placed by the county foster families ser-
vice, repeatedly the promise was made that her
father would never injure her again, never never
injure her again, she would be protected from him
forever and these words were proffered as a gift,
you understood that from the self-importance of
the statement, the swimmingness in the women's
eyes, thus Kathleen cast her own eyes down at once
as if in homage, stricken by gratitude, by humility,

by relief, the tiny rosebud mouth retreating, the moony face unevenly mottled by a blush rising from her throat even as her pulse kicked *I love him, he's my daddy God damn you to hell: fuckers.*

Joseph Hennessy was locked away in the State Correctional Facility for Men at Jackson, Michigan, for how many years Kathleen didn't know, this was not the sort of knowledge she might know, legal and documented knowledge beyond the scope of her imagination. If she'd been told, she'd forgotten at once. It was a kind of humility. In any case the convictions carried with them sentences unfixed and ambiguous as wisps of smoke, *from three to five years, from ten to twenty-five years, from fifteen to thirty-five years,* who could understand such riddles?—and in time he would die there, at Jackson, in a knife fight with another inmate. Kathleen was never to see her father again but she remembered him vividly for years: at night, in her assigned bed, in one or another of the foster homes through which she was rotated— the Chesneys, the Deitches, the Sweetmans, the McClures: waking suddenly to see that swollen face descending upon her, the pop eyes, the wormy veins in the forehead, the fists bearing down upon her like horses' hooves—*Where is she? your mother? filthy lying cunt of a mother?*—and Kathleen smelled whiskey and puke catching her father's blows full in her face and in the soft cringing parts of her body unprotected inside her pajamas, like a baby she tried to crawl down beneath the covers to escape burrowing headfirst beneath the covers but that only made Daddy madder, resisting only made him madder, Mommy had said *You'll learn: better now than later* but still Kathleen tried to escape, and Daddy yanked her back by her legs almost lifting her he was so strong, *Oh Daddy don't please Daddy* she was a big girl for her age but crying now knowing not to expect mercy from those hands, baby-tears and baby-kicking only made Daddy madder and now he had a broken-off chair leg in his hand grunting as he stooped smacking her methodically on the buttocks, on her belly, on her breasts, on the side of her head, now straddling her his face swollen with rage, eyes popping, the effort wheezing and grunting he made when he and Mommy struggled together in their bed like drowning people, and Kathleen and Nola lay awake listening fearful and not daring to breathe until it was over and they could sleep, and Daddy was saying *You know where she is! you know where she is!* and now Nola was scrambling to get away and Daddy reached out for her lifting her in one hand, her little legs kicking, little body squirming like a monkey's as he slapped her, slapped slapped slapped her, Kathleen was dazed seeing the room afire, flames rising from the lamps, the lights, her own hair, she was tugging at Daddy's arm trying to make him let Nola go, Nola's voice rose *Oh Daddy no Daddy nooooo* rising in a thin scream and with no more effort than it might be required to flick away an annoying insect Daddy knocked Kathleen off him and against the wall stumbling against the television set that fell from its stand, and then Daddy stopped, cursing and panting and he threw the chair leg against the wall, went into the bathroom and after a moment Kathleen crawled over the nylon carpet to where Nola was lying bleeding from her mouth and nose crying, trying to get breath to cry, and Kathleen was thinking how Mommy had left her in charge of Nola she was Nola's big sister Mommy had kissed her and said *You: you take care of her* going out to where Mommy's friend was waiting in her car for her, Mommy's friend Jolene from the beauty parlor and Kathleen whispered to Nola *Be quiet, Nola be quiet be quiet quiet* but Nola didn't hear, crying like a baby now in high sharp thin wails, Kathleen was terrified that Daddy would rush back at them, her head ached so badly, she was bleeding from places more than she could name, but when she touched Nola Nola kicked out the way a cat might and there close by was Daddy in the bathroom with the door flung open running water hard from a faucet talking angrily to himself, talking to Mommy saying all he'd do to her when he got hold of her, *Bitch, cunt, lying cunt I'll tear your head off* the last time he'd slapped Kathleen her head rang and buzzed for days and Mommy said with that bitter little smile *You'll learn: better now than later* and now Mommy had gone away and left her, her and Nola, and Nola wetted the bed sometimes, she was lying on the carpet bleeding and snuffling gnawing on the nylon carpet and Kathleen was squatting over her on her plump bruised haunches feeling ants run over her skin, tiny fiery ants, yes and bugs in her hair making her scalp itch too and prickle now Mommy was gone and Nola cried and cried like a baby her face wet with tears and snot and blood trickling from her nose and Kathleen was begging *Be quiet! be quiet!* and then she was shaking Nola in a sudden rage *You! Damn you! You will, will you! You will, will*—and Nola screamed and kicked at her as Kathleen straddled her banging her head against the floor, her silly little head, coconut-head, head like a damn dumb doll's, Kath-

leen had gotten her lice from Nola *she knew*
now that Mommy had gone away *and she hated
Mommy too* and the rage came over her like fire
so she could scarcely see how she gripped Nola's
head banging it hard and methodically against
the floor to quiet her, *You will, will you! Oh you
will*—and then she was banging Nola's head
against the sharp edge of the mattress support,
that sharp corner-edge Kathleen was always scrap-
ing her tender shin against and at once, with
astounding abruptness, Nola stopped screaming,
went limp, her little body limp, like a trick, like
she was playing, like the television picture disappearing when you turned off the power, whatever was there, whatever life, agitation, color,
human voices, music, all that disappearing into
emptiness that wasn't even emptiness but a shiny
glass surface, nothing profound, nothing actual
you might draw your fingertips against bemused
and wondering where that life had gone because
you knew you could never figure it out really,
where it had gone, or why, having been there at
all, so splendidly, it should so immediately and
so without resistance disappear.

Four

Mrs. Chesney's first name was Miriam which
drove out the name of Kathleen's mother though
sometimes in certain weathers like hazy humid
sunshine following rain or at dusk when it isn't
true dark and the lights come on but isn't true day-
light either Kathleen might see her mother: walking on the sidewalk, or ahead of her and Miriam
Chesney in the IGA pushing a shopping cart, lots
of times in cars passing by but she knew it wasn't
her mother really thus sucked in her mouth, looked
quickly away, said not a word. "—What a sad
sweet child you are," Miriam Chesney might sigh,
her cigarette uptilted in her mouth as she reached

out a lazy hand to brush Kathleen Hennessy's hair, her no-color hair that was always oily, a day after she shampooed it it was oily, out of the girl's face. Kathleen stood passive, with that meekness and stolidity of a young cow suffused with the heat of her own flesh, a secret stubbornness in the legs, the thighs, the haunches, even in the soft droopy breasts now nearly the size of Mrs. Chesney's so Mrs. Chesney would give her a quick intimate smiling-teasing look and say, "God, sweetie!—are you growing out of that bra *already?*" and the very word "bra" would make Kathleen blush.

She knew herself Mrs. Chesney's favorite among the children from the county, she basked in her special status.

It was like with Betty Lou at the hospital and that other nice nurse what was her name: Hazel. Regarding her with their motherly eyes, unjudging and warm, bringing her treats.

Especially in the kitchen together working side by side or in the cellar doing the laundry or shopping in the IGA or Sears or Woolworth's Mrs. Chesney and Kathleen Hennessy were alike as mother and daughter, wide-hipped, big-breasted, low-slung with legs that appeared foreshortened in the calf. And feet not large: size 5-B. And that look of no bones inside their flesh. They both liked babies which was a good thing because the Chesneys took in babies too, as young as four months sometimes. Mrs. Chesney said, sighing, expelling smoke, "—These damn little girls have their babies and somebody else has got to clean up the mess, uh-huh!—'The buck stops here.'" You had to know Miriam Chesney outside and in to know this was uttered not as complaint but as a statement of proud practical fact.

Though in other ways Kathleen and Mrs. Chesney were unalike. The older woman was darkish-skinned with swirls of pigmentation in her face and forearms, stippled tattoolike constellations of very dark freckles or moles, not disfiguring but oddly attractive, and attractive too was Mrs. Chesney's faint downy mustache on her upper lip, and her wide thick lips always colored a glossy deep maroon—lipstick applied first thing in the morning even on days sure to be "nothing" days. Her short perky hair was the color of root beer and tightly permed in tiny curls smelling faintly of beauty salon chemicals and this fact too, Mrs. Chesney's special smell or smells, mixed up with her perpetual cigarettes and her Arid underarm deodorant and an odor of kitchen grease and cleanser, helped to drive out the perfumy scent of Kathleen's mother, it was a fact of life Kathleen

Hennessy was beginning gradually to perceive how one thing drove out another, earlier thing, how you could not maintain two thoughts simultaneously but grew weak and exhausted with the effort, and no effort was worth it, and there was Mrs. Chesney running her fingers through Kathleen's hair as she did with the others simply as a way of establishing the fact that *Here I am, there you are* as she breezed through a room or clumped on the stairs, sometimes a quick chiding pinch of the cheek or the rear, a playful tickle in passing, that was how the Chesneys were at home, how they wanted you to be: no secrets: everything out in the open and tidy and self-evident as the Formica top of the kitchen table where they ate their meals, the gang of them.

Sometimes there were as many as six children from the county at the Chesneys' but most of the time only five.

And there was Mrs. Chesney's son from her first marriage Tiger who was twenty-six years old living at home but he behaved sometimes like one of the children especially teasing and bullying especially certain of the girls.

Mrs. Chesney admitted she was a sucker for any hard-luck story, sometimes accepting an emergency case over the telephone if it involved an infant—

"They always call me first, the sons of bitches." If she accepted an emergency case without consulting with Mr. Chesney there'd be surely an argument.

Mostly, though, the Chesneys didn't argue, and Mrs. Chesney maintained peace in the household except now and then teasing got out of hand, teasing and hyena-loud laughing around the supper table.

When Kathleen Hennessy first arrived at the Chesneys' it seemed to her in her fright and confusion that she was one of the younger children so she would keep that vague unexamined idea for the approximate two years of her stay with the family and when so abruptly she had to leave it was a puzzle to her that she was one of the older children in the family. She would not feel that she herself had changed in that interim, rather others had changed about her.

Her initial months at the Chesneys' she made a true effort to have feelings for the other children as if they were her brothers and sisters by blood now that her baby sister Nola was gone but as time passed, and the children came and went, she lost that impulse. The county placed children with foster families but the placements were often temporary: relatives sometimes appeared to make their claims or mothers released from prison or the state hospital demanded the return of their children and the law tended to be sympathetic with their demands, no matter how Mrs. Chesney pleaded and sometimes raged with the injustice of it, that a defenseless child must be returned to an unworthy mother, an alcoholic, or a drug addict, or a whore, any type of lowlife white trash favored over her because she was only a "foster" mother. In one of her moods she'd light up a cigarette and exhale smoke in a furious blue cloud, saying, "The things I know! Jesus God, the things I *know!*"

One day Kathleen saw Mrs. Chesney in the driveway talking with her mother who was wearing the same dress and her hair in the same shoulder-length style she'd worn it that day when she drove off with her friend Jolene in Jolene's rust-flecked convertible but when she looked a second time of course it wasn't her mother, Kathleen hadn't let on for an instant what she'd seen.

She wasn't sly or secretive as certain of the other girls said, jealous of her special relationship with Mrs. Chesney. She was quiet, though. "Biding her time"—whatever that meant.

Sometimes she stared at Mrs. Chesney when Mrs. Chesney wasn't aware, or perhaps Mrs. Chesney was aware, in a way: Kathleen would hear her say to someone in her droll singsong voice, "See her, that one?—'me and my shadow.'"

At the Chesneys' Kathleen Hennessy worried about eating too much, going out of control eating eating eating until her stomach burst but she worried too about not getting enough to eat at the supper table, the heavy bowls of food going around and everybody dipping in. Her color was improving, though. Her skin was still blemished in places but her color was much better, Mrs. Chesney said so. Soon after she came to live with the Chesneys her hair grew in nicer than before bushy and pale blond-brown like wood shavings and inclined to be oily but nice and thick with a wave and she'd stand wordless in a bliss of oblivion as Mrs. Chesney, cigarette uptilted in her mouth, brushed it vigorously to get out the snarls. Now Kathleen never remembered having a shaved head, the shame of it, the strange touch against her fingertips, nothing reminded her of it except sometimes happening to see Mr. Chesney's head in a certain light, how thin his hair was, thinner than her own father's, the pink shiny scalp peeking through. But really there was no need to remember. That was the happiness of so much bustle and commotion and noise at the Chesneys'. No need to remember, nor any need to recall her weeks in the hospital which were not all that unusual, Kathleen Hennessy wasn't a freak since other children in the foster home had often been hospitalized too, one fact cancels out another, one memory cancels out another, but a wave of mingled pleasure and regret would come over her if she saw a nurse on television for instance, a nurse's photograph in the newspaper, she'd speak out with uncharacteristic avidity so the others might glance at her as if a chair or a door had spoken, "Oh!—that's what I'm going to be, a nurse."

It was a statement of utter innocence made without volition and once when Kathleen made it gazing damp-eyed at the television screen in the Chesneys' living room one of her foster sisters laughed and said meanly, "Yeh but you got to graduate from high school first, dummy, that ain't gonna be easy for *you*," and Mrs. Chesney spoke up quickly, "—Shut up, you, what the hell do you know," later assuring Kathleen who was mute with shame that she could certainly be a nurse if she worked hard, that was the secret in school, working hard, she had years and years to go, didn't she, she was only in seventh grade now and doing well—"The thing is, not to be discouraged."

Kathleen was not doing well in school, in fact she was doing poorly, her worst subject was arithmetic but she had trouble writing too, moving her pen so slowly across the paper she forgot what she was trying to say like riding a bicycle so slowly you toppled over and she had trouble riding a bicycle too: her knees bumped together, the handlebars weaved from side to side. She was not doing well in school but it was a kind thing to be told she was, especially in front of the others.

Kathleen *was* Mrs. Chesney's favorite. Most of the time.

Except for the babies: but they shared the babies.

Except too for Mrs. Chesney's occasional spells of bad temper which no one could predict. At such times Mr. Chesney kept out of her way. He was a big burly heavy-footed man with a habit of screwing his face up in a wink, a good-natured guy as he called himself, worked for the city in Parks & Recreation driving a truck but if he got provoked into a quarrel voices would be raised, slaps and blows might be exchanged, kitchen utensils flung. Everyone from Tiger on down to the youngest toddling children knew to stay out of the Chesneys' ways if either had been drinking.

Miriam Chesney was partial to beer and sweet Gallo wine, Harry Chesney was partial to ale, Jesus that man could drink a case of ale in two days, sometimes less. You sure did stay out of his way.

Once Kathleen happened to come upon Mrs. Chesney in the upstairs bathroom where Mrs. Chesney was shaking something in her hand, a wad of bloody toilet paper, and she began screaming in Kathleen's face, "—I'm fifty-two years old for Christ's sake when am I going to be through with this!—bleeding bleeding bleeding like a stuck pig for eight fucking days now!" and Kathleen shrank away too astonished to be frightened, ran away to hide sucking her thumb and when she returned a few hours later it was like nothing had happened, that was Miriam Chesney's way.

Mrs. Chesney's laughter was rich and low like a man's and that had the effect too of canceling out Kathleen's mother's laughter which was breathy and hushed, almost silent at times, you'd have to look close to know was she laughing at all, or making another kind of sound.

Kathleen laughed infrequently and was not comfortable laughing, even with the Chesneys who liked to joke but especially at school. It seemed wrong somehow, a violation of etiquette, that certain of her teachers should say things calculated to make the students *laugh*. A sound like surprise would escape Kathleen and too late she'd clap her hand over her mouth looking to see if anyone had noticed, and once in the cafeteria a teacher said meaning to be kind, "Your teeth aren't ugly, Kathleen—really," so she was made to realize her teeth were ugly, all along they'd been ugly and she had not known others knew.

In school she rarely spoke hoping only not to be noticed or called upon for answers she could not give even when now and then she knew what they were, at home she spoke in a low careful voice as if she were fearful of stammering (for sometimes she did stammer) and she had phrases she said often in response to questions often asked, for instance "I don't mind if I do" was a frequent remark of Kathleen's, politely and even gravely uttered, when Mrs. Chesney asked would she be willing to do one or another household chore, even to get down on her hands and knees and scrub the filthy kitchen or hall or bathroom floor with steel wool, "—I don't mind if I do" Kathleen would say, and it was true, so true, no wonder Mrs. Chesney called the girl a dream, a sweetheart, a saint, "my right-hand man," but it was amusing too because if Mrs. Chesney asked Kathleen would she like a soda or how about joining her for a ride down to the shopping center Kathleen would reply in that same polite grave voice, "I don't mind if I do." As if she feared showing enthusiasm might cause the very object of her enthusiasm to vanish like a cruel magic trick.

Would she like to change little Barry's diaper?—"I don't mind if I do."

Would she like to scour out the oven, fouled with spilled-over macaroni-and-cheese casserole?—"I don't mind if I do."

Would she like a bite of this sugar doughnut?—"I don't mind if I do."

Would she like to go for a Sunday drive out to Belle Isle?—"I don't mind if I do."

When they laughed at Kathleen Hennessy their laughter was sometimes like tickling, Kathleen writhed with the delight of it, like an infant's her entire body was suffused with pleasure, but at other times their laughter was jeering, jabbing, like hard malicious fingers in her ribs or between her legs or one of the older boys at school pinching her breasts, the very nipples twisted and scorned. At the supper table when Tiger teased her, when Mrs. Chesney didn't intervene, and up and down the crowded table they laughed, Kathleen endured the torment sitting mournful and still at her place trying to chew her food, her slow jaws grinding food meant to be delicious now tasteless as paper, blinking tears from her eyes, it was because of Kath-

leen's soft drowning eyes that Tiger liked to tease
her, bringing out the color in her face, what a sad
mutt she is Tiger said, that kicked-dog look so you
naturally want to give her another kick, Tiger in
his soiled T-shirt and jeans and slicked-back cop-
pery hair but Mr. Chesney too could be in one
of his loud jokey jovial moods, bullying, hurtful,
but of course they called it "just kidding around"
and Mrs. Chesney too sometimes laughed, tears
streaking her darkish-powdered cheeks, Tiger pro-
tested to Mr. Chesney, "Don't be an asshole, asshole: I mean 'Dad,'" the two of them overgrown
louts needling each other red in the face and sometimes a glass might be overturned, or a bottle of
ale, a plate of food tumbling to the floor amid
shrieks, when Tiger was flying high he'd have the
entire table in stitches, even Mrs. Chesney smoking as she ate, and sipping beer too, and Kathleen
in a tumult of dread and wonder and sheer child-
ish giggling hiding her ugly teeth behind her
hand, Tiger would tell crazy tales of something
that had happened at work—he worked too in
Parks & Recreation: road maintenance—laughing
so hard sometimes he'd dribble food onto his
shirt or snort it up into his nose so Mrs. Chesney
pounded him on the back saying, "You damn fool:
you're gonna choke," and to the others, her lip-

sticked mouth wide in angry delight, "Jesus, you ever seen such a nut?—crazy damn fool?" It was clear though that Mrs. Chesney loved Tiger, you could never hope to come between them.

Tiger played parcheesi sometimes with the children, hunched over the board with a cigarette in his mouth. Kathleen liked the dice games best: you shook the dice, you saw what they added up to, you moved your piece around the board: no possibility of error.

With card games, gin rummy and black jack that were Mrs. Chesney's favorites, too much could go wrong. Sometimes Kathleen sat with a card in her fingers just staring at it, queen of spades? or was it clubs? what value had it, added together with the other cards in her hand? What did the other cards mean, ace of hearts, three of diamonds, that angry-looking king was he a king of spades or clubs, how did you keep them straight?—until they took the cards from her and shuffled them again not inviting her to play.

In her seat at school, buttocks like soft foam rubber. There was a girl who resembled Nola in a desk ahead, two desks over, just the side of her face and her hair in a limp pony tail and it was so strange a fact of life but a fact nonetheless: one thing cancels out another.

You learn not to look back, anything you're walking away from.

You don't cry. If you do, it isn't you.

She'd overheard Mrs. Chesney on the telephone drawling to a friend, "—This one, this one I told you about, the sort of moony one, twelve years old but looks like, Jesus, maybe sixteen, not bad-looking except her skin's broken out, poor thing, they were trying to say she was retarded but it's just she's scared I think, Christ wouldn't you be scared if, yeh, Christ it's a hard life, I could tell you some things!—but this one she's sweet, she's sort of I guess strange—just needs love I guess, needs time to get, y'know, adjusted."

Sometimes a child disappeared at midday which was when they came to get you from the agency. That's when *you know not to look back at anything you're walking away from.*

Power resided within her, though. A match lighted in a strategic place, at night . . . you saw plenty of fires on television. Some of them were fictitious fires and some were actual fires on the Detroit news programs: almost every night in the summer you heard the wailing sirens, their secret yearning sound.

They don't mean to be cruel, they're just teasing you because they're fond of you, Mrs. Chesney said. Running her fingers through Kathleen's thick bushy hair or her knuckles hard with affection over her head.

Tiger doesn't mean any harm, he's just—Tiger.

Once when Kathleen had been with the Chesneys only a few weeks she'd been hiding away in the bathroom with the door locked contemplating Betty Lou's gift, that lovely crystal rosary that meant beads of prayer—Mrs. Chesney had told her that, those very words: "beads of prayer"— when someone banged on the door and she opened it and there stood Tiger grinning down at her, his blunt bright eyes and wide jaw and T-shirt soiled under the arms and the front of his trousers unzipped.

Later, Kathleen could not have said how many days or weeks later, she glanced up to see him strolling through the upstairs of the house only the two of them there and he was whistling through his teeth, slicking his oiled hair back from his face with both hands and again the front of his trousers unzipped. Kathleen had stood very still her eyes narrowed not in apprehension nor even in distaste but in simple wariness for if she looked away that would acknowledge that she was looking. Tiger whistled through his teeth thinly and said in his low nasal jokey voice, ". . . Oh Kathleen: Kath-*leeeen* . . ." as if he were calling a dog.

Now Kathleen knew the understanding between them could never be altered because Tiger would be very angry and merciless in his torment of her. At the supper table she would sit chewing paper pulp blinking tears from her eyes as the others laughed.

Months passed, perhaps years. Yet Kathleen's anxiety about food at meal times, at least at supper times, did not subside. She sat at her place watching fixedly as the heavy bowls and platters were passed from hand to hand around the rectangular table, meatloaf, Salisbury steaks, canned tuna casserole, spaghetti with Mrs. Chesney's special sauce, ham steaks, macaroni and cheese, rice, potatoes, steamed spinach, puddings, Jell-O, pies from the bakery and pies Mrs. Chesney and Kathleen had baked, and her breath came quick and shallow watching in dread of the food running out before it reached her, and it never did, at least on the first serving; but often on the second. *Dear God let there be enough,* Kathleen would pray in silence—*please let there be enough* and if there was enough she did not then pray not to be teased, not to be tormented, reasoning that God had extended His kindness far enough for that occasion.

Sometimes a sensation as of ants rippled across her skin, her scalp shivered and prickled and she knew there was something that must be done, something pent-up like the air before an electrical storm that must be discharged otherwise she could not sleep. But if she jammed her fingers in her mouth and bit down hard enough she could contain it.

One of the babies was taken away by his father's mother and Mrs. Chesney got drunk and threw things around the kitchen and when Kathleen came in—she told herself, solemn and brave as a person, an adult, in a movie: *Don't be afraid*—she looked as if she was going to hit Kathleen but ended up hugging her instead. Hard. So hard.

But another baby came, in a few weeks, and it was so, as Kathleen had come to believe: one baby canceled another out. Like when you stare into a fire it is always the same fire and it is always the same moment for what fires teaches you is *what is, is now*.

She said: "That's what I'm going to be—a nurse."

Mrs. Chesney squinted against the drifting smoke from her cigarette. "Sure you are, honey. I know it and you know it."

When Kathleen was only a few days into eighth grade there came a new baby to the Chesney family, about six months old, malnourished, a tiny squawky thing with tufts of Indian-black hair and a capacity for tireless crying and threshing about in his crib and Kathleen loved to hold him more than anything else, Kathleen loved to bathe him and feed him even to change his diaper which needed changing often because he was sick in that part of him but quietly and gravely her face suffused with pleasure she would murmur, "Oh—I'll do it, I don't mind if I do," then standing there swaying humming to the baby laying the side of her warm cheek against his in a trance of oblivion. Every time she was told this baby's name she forgot it, thus called him "Baby" which was sufficient.

His mother had been a seventeen-year-old heroin addict, part Indian, from the Upper Peninsula. Got mixed up with a drug-dealing crowd in Detroit and died in the Detroit House of Correction for Women but Kathleen had a story she told herself, that Baby was hers: her Baby. He'd pushed out from between her legs from that secret place up inside her (she'd seen drawings of it, diagrams in the *Collier's Encyclopedia* at the public library) meaning he was *hers*.

But: one evening as she was lifting him from his bath he squirmed and kicked in her arms and the sensation as of ants, fiery ants, ran over her skin, startled she whispered, "—Oh Baby no: that's bad," yet Baby persisted, his small red face contorted in rage and his tiny fists flailing, there was his tiny penis bobbing between his legs like a fist too and Kathleen Hennessy stood paralyzed not knowing what to do and though her expression was unreadable and her eyes betrayed nothing so much as a profound and unarticulated astonishment it is possible that Mrs. Chesney who'd just entered the room knew by instinct what the situation was so without an instant's hesitation she took Baby from Kathleen's arms, simply stepped over her face screwed up against smoke drifting from her cigarette, murmuring something vaguely admonitory that might have been "Uh-uh" or "Oh no" which neither heard or would recall afterward: and there so suddenly was Mrs. Chesney crooning to Baby, wrapping him in a big soft white towel rocking and petting him until by degrees his crying subsided, and his frenzied kicking, and Kathleen fetched his formula, and he was fed with no further upset, and put to bed as usual.

And Mrs. Chesney who seemed not quite herself, vague and embarrassed, not looking at Kathleen, said "—Jesus God: wait till you get one of your *own*."

She'd had three actual babies, Mrs. Chesney told

Kathleen who appeared to be listening. Three "live births" of which Tiger was the youngest. And one miscarriage . . . did Kathleen know what a miscarriage was?

Kathleen who was perspiring and whose soft sallow moon-shaped face looked as if it had been slapped made a lateral movement of her head, possibly yes and possibly no, or perhaps she had not heard the question and Mrs. Chesney did not pursue the subject.

This was in March 1963 a week before the fire.

You could add up your life like a column of numbers like arithmetic on the blackboard: meaning . . . ?

The most puzzling remark Mrs. Chesney ever uttered in Kathleen's hearing was made two days before the fire, they were in the kitchen cleaning up after supper, Kathleen and Mrs. Chesney and a girl new to the family, a skinny silent frightened girl of ten, Rose Ann, veins so prominent at her forehead and wrists they seemed living things, the television was turned up loud in the other room and Mrs. Chesney banging things in the sink, splashing soapy water on the counter and smoking her perpetual cigarette scarcely minding if ash fell into the sink, must have been listening to the tele vision—Kathleen was not: Kathleen was not listening to anything, anyone at all—since she burst into laughter suddenly, her rich low belly-laughter like a man's, and said, "—Just what I'm thinking: next time around I'm gonna come back as something real tough, rubbery like a Goddamn *toad*. See what the fuckers can do to me *then*."

She laughed so, in her contagious way, both Kathleen and Rose Ann joined in. Though they were bewildered.

They *were* bewildered, but separately. Kathleen had long since learned (though she'd forgotten the precise stages of her learning) that such moments of overlapping emotion even quick poignant exchanges of glances, a knuckly hand rubbed with rough affection across a head, were not real really. Not really.

Then came the fire, and all that followed.

And Kathleen Hennessy, now thirteen years old, and the other surviving children, were placed with new foster families in the area: Kathleen went to a family named Deitch on the east side which lasted only three months (Mr. Deitch was arrested for drunken driving) then with the Sweetmans in Ferndale beyond Nine Mile Road where Kathleen might have remained until she came of age and was no longer the responsibility of the county but Mrs. Sweetman had a kidney infection that worsened until she was hospitalized so once again Kathleen was reassigned and this final time to a family named McClure who lived on Brush Street near Vernor and who did not seem to care for her as if judging her beforehand: though by this time Kathleen was fifteen years old, in tenth grade, her brassiere size 36-C, her skin less noticeably blemished but encrusted with makeup and her rosebud-mouth a glossy luminous pink. Mrs. McClure was a nervous woman whose smiles seemed to pinch her face; a tall reedy-voiced middle-aged woman with glistening-gray hair in a tight perm that fitted her head like a cap and a habit of exhaling smoke in angry bluish clouds so she canceled out Mrs. Chesney, or what remained of Mrs. Chesney. By then Mrs. Chesney was a long time ago.

The fire: it had come with no warning in the night, everyone in the Chesneys' house was asleep.

By the time the first fire truck arrived at 3:20 a.m. the entire second floor of the old woodframe house on Eleventh Street was ablaze.

FOUR, ONE AN INFANT,
PERISH IN EAST SIDE BLAZE

—this was the headline in the Detroit *Free Press* for March 22, 1963, with an accompanying photograph on the first page of the metropolitan section of the paper. It was stated that the probable cause of the fire had been a smoldering cigarette in a clump of oily rags in a closet. Who exactly was to blame, whose cigarette it might have been, was not revealed. And in the smudged-looking photograph the Chesneys' house might have been any burning house, no way to identify it.

Even a photograph of poor quality of a fire teaches *whatever is, is now:* all else canceled out.

Kathleen was asleep, or nearly, in her bed at the upstairs rear of the house when the smell first came to her, unmistakable, scorch, heat, something damp meanly burning like paper or rags, she was lying very still on her back as always her rosary twined in her fingers (which was how Kathleen put herself to sleep each night cherishing her "beads of prayer" moving her lips silently not in prayer exactly because she was uncertain of the words but words of her own invention) when the smell made her nostrils pinch and her eyes begin to smart yet for a strange moment she remained unmoving as if paralyzed or asleep as if mistrusting whether this might be a dream for so much happened in the crowded interior of her skull both by day and by night she had learned to be wary *Is it real? is it real—really?* for you can be mocked cruelly if you confuse one with the other.

Kathleen shared her room with the ten-year-old Rose Ann, each had a cot for a bed and there was a space of perhaps ten inches between the cots. Always afterward it would be said that Kathleen Hennessy had saved Rose Ann Dwyer's life, long after Kathleen herself had pushed away the memory Rose Ann Dwyer would cherish it for who among us can point with absolute unerring confidence to a point in time and to a specific agent the intersection of which resulted in the prolongation of our existences?—who among us can affix to a reified fate an actual human face?—though in the initial confusion Kathleen seemed to have forgotten Rose Ann entirely as she ran to wake up the others, calling for Mrs. Chesney, screaming Mrs. Chesney's name as if help might come from that part of the house where the fire had most fiercely taken hold: and how quickly it had taken hold as if like a meteor it had dropped from the sky or had it been waiting for years slyly biding its time in the very woodwork of the old house, in the very plasterboard and carpeting: but waves of smoke beat her back, waves of terrible heat as of an immense oven so she retreated, ran to get the other girl cowering in her bed and pulled her, this girl, this girl whose name she could not have said, out of her bed, out of the path of the fire and half-carried her down the back stairs the two of them sobbing and whimpering like terrified animals even after they were outside, and safe.

There, it was winter: snow crunching underfoot and Kathleen realized she was barefoot, in her pajamas her breasts loose, naked inside her flannel pajamas while above her the house burned, waterfalls of angry flame rose vertically into the air and the noise! the roaring! as of maddened winds! and those screams from the second floor! and Kathleen was running in the street screaming for help and someone seized her to wrap a coat or a blanket around her even as she struggled to get away, and within minutes the first of the fire trucks arrived, there were police vehicles, an ambulance, sirens, flashing lights, the ladders from the fire trucks were swung erect and the great hoses activated and Kathleen crouched with her fingers jammed in her mouth staring entranced as the fire illuminated the now unrecognizable house from within like a gigantic breath *You fuckers: now you see* and the firemen were large shiny insects drawn by the heat and beauty of the fire but powerless against it so long as she watched for where streams of water from their hoses beat flames back at one window or at one patch of shingled roof the flames retreated only to reappear elsewhere billowing outward with doubled ferocity and when a medical worker came to lead her away she resisted, digging her bare heels into the snow, calling suddenly for Mrs. Chesney, screaming Mrs. Chesney's name, screaming "No no no no *no*" until she was lifted, struggling, a plump soft-bodied girl wearing only pajamas, her disheveled hair singed, her eyebrows and lashes singed, lifted and carried to an ambulance to be strapped down on a stretcher her screams mounting even as her mind was utterly blank and extinguished like a candle flame snuffed out by the flattened palm of a great merciful hand.

That was March 22, 1963 : after that night Kathleen Hennessy never knowingly saw again what remained of the house on Eleventh Street, nor any razed and rubble-strewn site where the house had stood. And had a new house been built where the old had stood she would perhaps not have recalled the exact location of the old house thus if in fact a new house was eventually built on that site she would not have taken note though for years—for the remainder of her lifetime in fact—she would continue to live in Detroit or in its vicinity often riding the city buses, occasionally as a passenger in a car but at such times her attention was likely to be distracted and in any case it was not Kathleen Hennessy's nature to brood thus if she chanced to see the former site of the Chesney house it was not knowingly.

PART *Two*

One

COUNT YOUR BLESSINGS: a needlepoint sampler in all the colors of the rainbow framed and hanging prominently behind the receptionist's desk at the Wayne County Department of Community Health.

COUNT YOUR BLESSINGS but Kathleen Hennessy was not one who must be told.

Years before Jesus Christ was welcomed into her heart Kathleen observed the custom of remembering in her nightly prayers those persons who had been kind to her.

Those others: she made an effort to forget.

Her crystal beads of prayer with the shiny miniature crucifix wound about her fingers as she dropped off to sleep . . . frequently so exhausted from work that sleep seemed instead to rise to her . . . jagged peaks, needle-sharp stalagmites rising to penetrate her consciousness and draw her down even as she prayed with a child's methodical precision *Thank you God for—. Thank you for—. Our Father Who art in Heaven thank you for—. And Jesus Christ Our Lord thank you—.*

Naming these persons clearly and distinctly as pebbles dropped in water, each pebble separate from the one preceding and the one following for Kathleen genuinely worried that should she fail to name these persons one by one God Himself would have no knowledge of them and they would sink into the same oblivion as those who had been hurtful of her whom she meant to forget.

At Warren P. Wilson High School there was Mrs. Feinberg who taught remedial English, who gently mocked Kathleen's shamefaced murmur *Oh I can't: I just can't* by mimicking her in comical exaggeration *Oh! I can't! oh oh! I just can't!* mimicking not only Kathleen's voice of infinite resignation and self-defeat but her mannerisms as well, her lowered head, rapidly blinking eyes, twitchy shoulder movements, forcing Kathleen to laugh startled as if a fun-house mirror had been thrust up in front of her forcing her to confront the fact as Mrs. Feinberg insisted that she was her "own worst enemy" so mysteriously lacking confidence in herself when she could write as well as anyone in the class when she was among the more intelligent students in the class thus to combat this enemy lurking inside herself Kathleen must answer her own *I can't* with Mrs. Feinberg's *Yes you can Kathleen: OH YES YOU CAN* and by God's grace in both her junior and senior years it was so for she was allowed to graduate with her class and would forever retain a good positive attitude toward reading if not toward writing which remained vexing to her not simply in execution but in theory: for why write, why take pen to paper, if you could speak more easily? why filter snarls of language through your finger's blundering tips if you could utter words easily, at least more easily?

And also at Warren P. Wilson there was Mrs. Moynahan who taught home economics and who gave even more of her time than Mrs. Feinberg to Kathleen Hennessy refusing to allow the girl to sell herself short to undervalue herself even to stand with rounded shoulders *Kathleen: come now: this is a watchbird watching YOU!* and who invited her to visit the home economics department after school so they could talk together in private, the two of them like mother and daughter preparing Ovaltine in the practice kitchen then sitting like ladies in the practice living room, Kathleen in a bliss of pleasure and privilege scarcely tasting the chalky drink listening eagerly to Mrs. Moynahan confide in her as no adult had ever done not even her foster mothers, talking of her girlhood in Detroit many years before and her own difficulties with teachers, classmates, parents: *The thing is Kathleen we must never never lose faith in ourselves for faith is everything.* And this too was true as Kathleen saw.

(Graduation day amid the crowd in her silly rented gown and mortarboard cap Kathleen had wanted to tell Mrs. Feinberg and Mrs. Moynahan how grateful she was to them, she'd wanted to take their hands in hers and kiss them whispering words she'd practiced countless times in secret *I love you* but of course she had not dared: she'd hung back, transfixed with shyness, gnawing like an overgrown baby at a thumbnail and so the opportunity passed, the precious opportunity passed, never to be repeated.)

And there were her friends at the Detroit Christian Youth Fellowship which met at the YM-YWCA especially Reverend Deck and his wife Penny both of them freckle-faced and smiling calling her Kathy at their very first meeting as if they'd known her all their lives and had been simply waiting to meet her, like Jesus Christ Himself as they explained waiting all her life for Kathleen Hennessy to open her heart to Him and it was *Jesus love you Kathy!* and *God love you Kathy!* smiling as they told her of the love and forgiveness and grace of God, the good news of the Gospels, Jesus Christ who died for her sins that she be washed pure as snow again and redeemed and her very body resurrected at Judgment Day at the end of Time, yes and the fires of Hell for them who refuse to believe who refuse to allow Jesus Christ into their selfish hearts for did Our Savior not say *I bring not peace but a sword?* and did He not say to the multitude who wished to stone the woman taken in adultery *He that is without sin among you, let him first cast a stone at her?* and did He not teach *Except as ye become like unto little children ye shall not enter the Kingdom of Heaven?* Most difficult for Kathleen Hennessy to grasp was the revelation put to her by Reverend Deck that Jesus loved her as no mortal man or woman could love her; that He forgave her her sins as no mortal man or woman could forgive her; that in the eyes of The Father it is the lame and the halt and the blind the downtrodden of mankind who are not only valued as others on earth but above these others for *the first shall be last, and the last first.*

Precious even above these was Nurse Bobbi McDermott of the Wayne County Department of Community Health who spoke so kindly to Kathleen when she applied for a position as a nurse's aide (not knowing of course that Kathleen had telephoned the Department numerous times during the past year always hanging up quickly before identifying herself) explaining the duties of a nurse's aide and the possibilities for employment in hospital and home care and the sort of training required by the State of Michigan, inquiring politely of Kathleen was she eighteen or over? did she have a high school diploma or its equivalent? what was her previous work experience?—would she be able to get letters of recommendation from employers, teachers, a minister or priest? was she willing to work with the seriously or terminally ill? the elderly? the mentally disabled? was she willing to "prepare" the dead when necessary?

was she in a position to take brief training courses in night school if the Department approved her application?

Bobbi McDermott was a handsome olive-skinned woman of about thirty with hair cut short rising to a crest like a blue jay's: talking of nursing and nursing care, her eyes fairly shone. She told Kathleen Hennessy that of all factors contributing to a desirable nurse or nurse's aide it was *attitude* that was most important: "For all people say, Miss Hennessy, it's the individual's God-given disposition that counts. You know—'actions speak louder than words.'"

Not at this initial meeting but the following week when Kathleen was assigned to her first job at Detroit Metropolitan Hospital did she dare to take Bobbi McDermott's hand in her own, upon impulse reaching out to actually seize the young woman's hand in an expression of childlike gratitude, breathless, smiling, blinking back tears, murmuring, "—Oh thank you Miss McDermott, oh—*I love you.*"

So saying her nightly prayers Kathleen named these persons, and some others. Those others she could recall. Fearing that without her intervention

God would indeed overlook them as seemingly on this earth at least He overlooked so many. *I stood before them, oh and I was not ugly or clumsy like a cow but seeing me they saw my soul like a shimmering flame they did not see me in the flesh at all but another standing where I stood: Praise God.*

Two

Just as years before in an interlude in her life now virtually forgotten Kathleen Hennessy as a child of eleven had come to unexpected bloom in a ward at Children's Hospital so now as a young woman of nineteen did she come to a yet more radiant bloom as a nurse's aide at Detroit Metropolitan Hospital where she was trained in such matters as *handwashing procedures* which came to fascinate her to the point very nearly of trance as if she believed that such procedures as instructed by her superiors were clues to a fundamental principle of the universe both the human world so difficult to comprehend let alone negotiate and the world beyond the human hitherto wholly incomprehensible, unfathomable thus in a sort of waking trance a small pinched smile on her face eyes lowered as if in tremulous reverence she obeyed every commandment of such matters as *handwashing procedures*—

> *As the insides of sinks are considered*
> *contaminated use levers operated only*
> *by the foot, knee, or elbow to regulate*
> *water supply and cleaning agent.*
> *Adjust water flow to WARM.*
> *Wet hands liberally.*
> *Apply generous amount of soap.*
> *Working up a lather be sure to concentrate*
> *on web spaces between fingers. Lather for 20*
> *seconds.*
> *Rinse thoroughly, holding hands downward.*
> *Rinse again.*
> *Dry hands thoroughly with clean paper towel.*
> *Replace soap on pronged soap rest (never in*
> *dish).*
> *Turn faucet off with clean paper towel.*
> *ENTIRE PROCEDURE REQUIRES*
> *APPROXIMATELY 1 MINUTE.*

—for it was impressed upon the nurse's aides that in a hospital all personnel no matter their rank and all patients no matter their diagnoses are recognized as potential carriers of pathogenic organisms *bacteria viruses rickettsia fungi worms protozoa* thus personal hygiene of the most scrupulous sort was demanded of all: daily bathing at home and shampooing of hair, spotlessly clean uniforms, underwear, stockings, shoes, thorough washing of hands following the hospital procedure after each encounter with a patient or routine work in the patient area, yes and a powerful germicide-detergent solution was to be used after the performing of certain tasks namely the bathing of patients, clean-up of patient area, removal of food trays and bedside paraphernalia and bedpan-urinals . . . indeed it was ABSOLUTELY NECESSARY that all bedpan-urinals be rinsed with cold water, scrubbed with a toilet brush and germicide-detergent solution, then rinsed again and boiled for no less than thirty minutes. Alone among the new nurse's aides Kathleen Hennessy grasped immediately and with an air of satisfaction the logic that a true aura of Death cloaked the heedlessly Living; that invisible enemies sought entry ceaselessly at all human orifices just as, as Reverend Deck warned, the Devil ceaselessly sought entry into the purest and most innocent of souls *thus one could never be too vigilant.*

Yet what joy—surely it shone in her face? her eyes? the glisten of her skin?—in learning the proper procedure at last for making beds; ten steps for the unoccupied bed, nineteen for the occupied; in learning the proper procedure for giving a patient a bath, out of bed or in; in learning the proper procedure for moving and positioning patients—ambulatory patients, bed-rest patients, patients unable to move of their own volition, unconscious or comatose patients. It gave her pleasure to assist a patient at mealtimes and naturally it gave her most pleasure when a patient ate well, and with appetite; she never failed to report to the nurse those patients who were eating poorly. And she who for years had hurriedly and even grudgingly brushed her teeth averting her eyes in shame from her mirrored image now took satisfaction in brushing the teeth of patients incapable of brushing their own, cleaning their mouths thoroughly, cleaning dentures when required, for it was a sudden revelation to her that no mouth was ugly in itself no matter how misshapen, no matter how crooked or decayed the teeth: no face, no body, no being.

Praise God. For all is His handiwork.

So when an elderly woman burst into tears one day when Kathleen was bathing her, saying, in a faint broken voice, "I wasn't always like this, once

I was young as you," Kathleen said, confused, "Oh—but God loves us all," and reached out to squeeze the woman's hand. And they remained like that in that position for some seconds. *Praise God.*

There was a more subtle pleasure in learning to restrain unruly or delirious patients tying them for their own protection by their wrists and ankles to their beds; in preparing "mitts"—padded hand protectors—to prevent an irrational patient from pulling out IV needles, drainage tubes, urinary catheters, and the like. Sometimes patients *even adult men* screamed, or wept, or begged, "Don't hurt me!" their eyes snatching at Kathleen's and Kathleen was empowered to reassure them as if in another's calm steady superior voice, "Nobody is going to hurt you, please relax this is for your own good." Which was always true.

With the passage of weeks Kathleen began to realize that her powers of observation were sharpening; her senses were becoming more alert. Where in school—and how she had dreaded, detested school—dreaded, detested her classmates—she had been slow-witted and clumsy here in the hospital she was as intelligent as the other nurse's aides, oh she was certain—she was certain: for what pleasure in filling out patients' reports, noting on a checklist if a patient was *in pain,* or *looking ill,* or *fatigued,* or *looking well;* if a patient was *unconscious,* or *depressed,* or *restless,* or *responsive;* what was the frequency, quantity, and character of his "output" of *vomitus, urine, feces, drainage of wounds, catheters, tubes.* Little escaped her scrutiny. Her reports were neat and accurate. If a set of instructions gave her trouble she asked another aide for help and rarely did she ask the same favor twice. It seemed to her that a galaxy of wonders was opening before her, God's secrets blossoming before her very eyes, so much she had never known or guessed in her previous blind life.

She was thanked, she received compliments.

Many times in a single day she was told *Fine Kathleen!—you're catching on.*

She had friends among the nurse's aides. A friend or two among the nurses: the nice ones: Midge, Reena.

The male aides, the orderlies. Sometimes they smiled at her. Called her "Kathleen," even "Kathy." Even the younger doctors, the interns, the residents. Smiling sometimes at her. Or in her direction.

Never never lose faith in ourselves for faith is everything.

Usually, patients liked her. That would be so

through Kathleen Hennessy's career of several decades.

On the floor to which she was assigned at Detroit Metropolitan Hospital she quickly became known for: her reliability, her diligence, her good manners, her congenial uncomplaining nature, her ability to follow instructions if the instructions were spelled out clearly to her. Her energy. Her strong husky arms. Her shy fleeting smile. That startled sweetness breaking out of her face like a struck match.

True, at times she exasperated certain of the nurses. She could appear slow-witted, perhaps deaf. Dumb. Cow-clumsy with wide thick hamlike hips; that bosom heavy and sloping as that of a middle-aged woman. But her ankles were surprisingly slender, and her wrists. Often she carried herself with a sort of grace and pride moving efficiently noiselessly in her flawless white nurse's shoes. Her uniforms were fresh at least at the start of her shifts. Her stocking seams were straight. In mimicry of one of the popular young nurses she wore her hair braided and lopped and pinned about her head hidden neatly beneath her white starched cap. Her face was moon-shaped, chubby, her complexion mottled and slightly coarse but no longer visibly disfigured by acne and if there

remained tiny nicks and scars in her skin they
could be disguised by pancake makeup spread
poreless-thick and a layer of powder.

And Kathleen's prim little mouth—it was attractive now, and primed to smile. Carefully lip-
sticked in coral-pink, or orangish-red, or true red,
or, most glamorous of all, a deep dusky luscious
burgundy-grape. *Never never lose faith.*

"—her?—Hennessy?—she's a good kid—"
"—she's O.K. once you get used to her—"
"—not quick but not, y'know, stupid either—"
"—*is* she cross-eyed?—"
"—anyway she follows directions—"
"—oh but—" (laughter) "—poor thing!"
"—how old d'ya think?—a lot older than—"
"—nah she's younger actually, Connie says
twenty—"
"—twenty?—I don't believe it—"
"—*her?* Hennessy?—"
"—she *is,* Connie said—they were on the bus
together and got talking—"
"—Jesus, poor thing she's so—"
"—nah look: she's all right—"
"—her eyes, is she cross-eyed?—or what?—"

Crouched in the lavatory stall Kathleen felt her
face afire, her hair afire, heart beating so hard she

was in dread they could hear it and would discover her, but they went out laughing and alone she wiped tears from her eyes *Oh—but they like me don't they?—they are my friends aren't they?*

FECES FINGERS FLIES FOOD FLUIDS
—through her head certain words ran continuously like small prayers for which she Kathleen Hennessy was the vehicle merely—
FECES FINGERS FLIES FOOD FLUIDS
—for which praise God.

At last Death came for her.
She'd known she must one day find herself in the presence of Death, one day she must help to prepare a deceased patient for the morgue, yet when a patient expired virtually before her she was baffled as if a trick of some sort were being played upon her as a man had done once *sprawled legs and arms outstretched on Kathleen's own bed his tongue protruding and goofy eyes rolled back up into his head his trousers unzipped and red-veined Thing bobbing erect* thus she could not speak or comprehend staring at the motionless figure in the bed finally wetting her lips, "—Oh Mr.—, oh are you—are all right— Are you— Oh—" not knowing what she said knowing the

man must be dead, an emaciated cancer patient with a face like a crumpled rag, not old, yet not young, no-age, terrible to contemplate and she'd known of course that he was dying, it was understood he was dying yet now she wondered if there might be some mistake knowing she should not touch the body yet in a sudden panic she would be blamed for his dying she took hold of his hand— cool limp rubbery hand—said begging, "Oh please no—oh NO oh NO," beginning to cry in hoarse scared sobs stooped over the figure in the bed so wizened, bone-sharp, the eyes faint mucus-crescents beneath the lids, only a few piteous hairs on the scalp, queer liverish stains on the scalp, dentures prudently removed when the patient was moved to "the quiet room" as it was called off the open ward and they'd been cautioned to behave naturally to him and in his presence continuing to assure him that all was well that everything that could be done for him was being done even though already the patient appeared to be unconscious his mouth slack and sores glistening on his lips *Remember: the sense of hearing is present until the termination of life* so Kathleen Hennessy clearly understood that the man was dying, if questioned she'd have said yes that patient in that room is dying, for weeks he'd been attached to an indwell-

ing catheter voiding almost continuously in mi-
nuscule amounts of sharp-smelling urine and she'd
several times been asked to help bathe him and
to assist with an enema yet now she wept squeezing his dead hand in her living hands and in
this posture she was discovered by the floor nurse
who spoke at first sharply to her, "Kathleen," saying, "Kathleen!" then touching her shoulder, but
gently, as if to release her: so like an overgrown
baby she fled.

It was very early in the morning, a gauzy dawn,
how unfair Kathleen was thinking that a soul
should pass away at the very hour when a day
was beginning and when, in another wing of the
great hospital, new souls were being born.

She recalled suddenly the burning house, the
asphalt siding you would not think would burn
with such ferocity, like a comet fallen out of the
sky the house was ablaze and all who watched were
blameless, Kathleen Hennessy was surely blameless and never for a moment under suspicion and
perhaps in fact it had not been she who'd dropped
a lighted cigarette into a greasy rag so oddly
hidden away in a closet at the front of the house
perhaps it had been someone else entirely and even
that other party blameless before the spectacle of
God's wrath: of Death: and now hiding in the

women's lavatory like a coward and a fool in that smelly windowless room where in the mirror there floated big-breasted big-assed Kathleen Hennessy who dared not look at herself *Oh! I am so ashamed* hiding her face leaking tears though knowing full well (for had she not been instructed? many times? by her superiors, many times?) that her fingers were contaminated by germs and bacteria she decided suddenly, or did the resolve come to her from outside her, like a hand pressing hard between her shoulder blades, urging her, prodding her, yes she ran back to the patient's room and reported to Nurse Edith Myers that she was all right now, she was fine, she was ready to prepare the deceased, she was sorry she'd broken down like that but now she was ready: and it seemed to her a match flaring up in a darkened room how Nurse Edith Myers looked at her startled and smiling, saying, "Kathleen, are you sure? You look so pale. I can get someone else, if—"

Kathleen said quickly, "Oh—oh yes! Oh no!— I mean—*please don't get anyone else.*"

As, as in that twilit state neither sleep nor full wakefulness over the years from Detroit Metropolitan Hospital to the Twin Oaks Convalescent Home in Hamtramck to the Helene P. Olden

Foundation Clinic in Livonia to the St. Francis
of Assisi Rehabilitation Center again in Detroit
to the Greater Detroit Medical & Convalescent
Center to the Sunnyfield Nursing Home on Seven
Mile Road Kathleen Hennessy would find herself
in a succession of selves performing by rote with
unfailing confidence and always with satisfaction
these seemingly ancient rites pertaining to the
dead: to Death.

Procedure:

Obtain the Death Pack. (One wrapping sheet,
absorbent cotton, padding, bandage rolls,
safety pins, identification tags/death tags.)

Lower the headrest, leaving a single pillow.
Place the body in a natural position—arms at
sides, palms turned toward thighs.
Close eyelids gently.
Replace cleaned dentures (if necessary).
Close mouth gently.
Remove all treatment equipment from the
patient unit such as IV stand, oxygen, suction
equipment etc.

For removal: stretcher, sheets (2), litter
straps (2), laundry hamper, large paper bag.
DO NOT ENTER sign for door.

Remove all top bedding except for draping sheet.

Remove patient's pajamas.

Remove any drainage tubing, dressings, catheters.

Clean old adhesive markings from skin.

Press bladder gently to expel accumulated urine. Place cotton pads over rectum and genitalia to absorb feces and urine which will be expelled as sphincters relax.

Prop sagging jaw with folded pads.

Pad ankles with cotton and tie together with bandage.

Tie one signed tag to right great toe.

Tie second signed tag to left wrist.

Roll body gently to side of bed and place one clean sheet diagonally under the body.

Roll body back to center of sheet.

Fold upper corner of sheet loosely over the head and face, lower corner over the feet.

Secure the arms at the sides as the right and left corners of the sheet are brought over to complete the wrapping.

Fasten sheet with safety pins.

Fasten third signed tag to outside of sheet.

(If dentures could not be replaced, wrap in gauze, identify, and pin dentures next to tag.)

Lift wrapped body to stretcher.

Fasten litter straps at chest and just above knees.

Cover body with sheet.

Transfer body quietly and with dignity to the morgue.

Avoid if possible public entrances and lobbies.

Return with stretcher to floor.

Final cleaning of patient's unit and disposal of all contaminated material.

Three

Eyes followed her, often.

Eyes and hands, the gestures of hands. And lewd thoughts of lewd men.

In the rich bloom of her youth Kathleen Hennessy did not lack for, if not suitors precisely, male companionship of one kind or another: evening engagements on the average of one or two a week ranging from encounters at the Detroit Christian Youth Fellowship where in the gymnasium of the West Grand Boulevard YM-YWCA young men and women danced together to records on Friday evenings (and where once outside an exit door a thickset clammy-handed vocational arts teacher named Bill Brandt whispered, "I—I like you very m-much, Kathleen," and clumsily kissed her on the lips: but never after that evening spoke to her again for no reason the mortified young woman could guess) to blind dates arranged by certain of her charity-minded co-workers at the hospital (in whose cars speeding along late-night Detroit streets Kathleen Hennessy was often kissed, even caressed, fondled—dreamy beery sequences these were, wonderfully exciting yet rarely repeated) to actual dates arranged casually at bars, taverns, pizzerias, the hospital cafeteria where with the other young women yet unmarried thus available Kathleen Hennessy exhausted and giddy from her shift glanced covertly about to see was she being seen *Oh why not? why not me—'Kathleen'? Why do none of you see me?* and most of the time their eyes went through her not cruel or scornful simply not seeing as if her very substance, to her so fleshy, so blood-driven and urgent, so yearning, were invisible, and then unexpectedly when she'd given up hope it might happen that a young man or one not-so-young would drift in her direction, *Is he? is he? is he?* as if reluctantly staring at her as if drawn to her white uniform, the snug-fitting nylon white flush across Kathleen's large breasts more than one man had caressed in wonder murmuring *Beautiful!* and this too reluctantly as if the word were forced from him, ejaculated out of him like semen, the large soft drooping breasts like balloons filled with warm water, the swelling hips and belly, the moist smoothness of her pale gauzy stockings rubbing together at her plump knees, thighs. And sometimes afterward her flesh would yield bruises ripe as fruit in the shapes too of fruit, or teeth marks deep in the folds of her skin, the fatty creases of the belly and thighs prematurely wattling though she was young—still young: *young!*—waiting for her life, the life ordained for her by God, to begin. Sometimes in desperation she found herself alone or in the company of young women of doubtful character, slangy and foul-mouthed and there was Kathleen Hennessy among them smiling vague and somewhat frightened on a Saturday night in the Tip Top Café on Livernois where the races mingled, jostling on the dance floor in the sweaty heat and pulse of a live combo playing Chubby Checker music, Fats Domino, Little Richard, there was the Leaning Tower on Six Mile Road, Sal's Keyboard Lounge on the way to Belle Isle where they'd bring a bottle and where within earshot of the coarse lapping waves of the Detroit River Kathleen allowed certain things to be done to her, not to her precisely but to her body, heavy, passive, voiceless, yet grateful even for these seemingly anonymous acts, rough caresses that were still caresses, harsh kisses nonetheless kisses, so long as she did not resist she would not be hurt or insulted, or rarely so, and most of the time the men were willing to drive her back home to the shingleboard house on Second Avenue just below Highland Park where she rented a two-room apartment and she would not remember or would not remember much of what had happened, drunk and giggly as if being tickled stumbling on the stairs as if for the benefit of others in the house—other girls, women: hospital workers, secretaries, bank clerks unmarried too and keenly and jealously aware of one another's "dates"—and in her bathroom she'd sometimes force herself to vomit, liquor, food, semen, after the most convulsive heaves Kathleen always felt better like a patient suffering so from impacted feces and then the relief of the enema, the relief to the point of actual tears of the voiding of such foulness where foulness had turned to pain, was indistinguishable from pain: *Oh! forgive me, God!* Nearly always then she felt better, restored to herself except if she discovered what he'd done to her, silky underwear ripped, the soreness of her nipples, chafed tender flesh of the labia and vagina but what made her weep most despairingly one night a week after her twenty-second birthday in March 1972 when in fact she'd been out with a young resident from the hospital, one of those edgy-eyed young unmarried doctors drawn to the white uniforms of the nurses and the nurse's aides, yearning and contemptuous at once *Oh sure they're crazy for you sure they'll fuck you but they sure as hell won't marry you the arrogant sons of bitches, medical school hot shits but at least they use condoms* and he'd pulled out a chair beside her in the cafeteria asked would she like to go out for dinner sometime, drinks or whatever, he was on thirty-six-hour call until Sunday night then he'd have some time off maybe then? and Kathleen Hennessy heard these words through a haze of murmurous confusion that must have been blood dinning in her ears, she'd managed to stammer a reply blushing to the very roots of her hair, the young doctor's name was Orson Abbott and she had followed him with her eyes for a very long time not knowing his name and believing him so remote from her she would not have thought it worthwhile to learn his name, there at the hospital you quickly learned your rank, your place, your value which was interchangeable with that of any other nurse's aide thus humble and yet he'd come to her to her Kathleen Hennessy chosen above the others, he was aware of her too and speaking to her and of course she'd agreed to meet him that Sunday but there wasn't time for dinner in a restaurant only pizza slices devoured standing at a crowded bar and then in his car in Palmer Park he hadn't said much, mouth tight, eyes tight-seeming too behind his dark-framed glasses with their schoolboy look and it had happened between them wordless too and urgent but he'd fumbled with the condom, ejaculating groaning "Shit—oh shit" on Kathleen's skirt pulled above her crotch—what made her weep now so despairingly in her room unable to care if her neighbors overheard was the nasty dried clot of semen on her skirt, a gob of mucous in her black pleated wool skirt from Hudson's that was the most beautiful article of clothing Kathleen Hennessy had ever owned.

Yet it is promised: the first shall be last and the last, first.

In her white rubber-soled shoes she kept spotlessly clean out of pride in her white uniform spotless too at least at the start of her shift how silently how capably she passed among them, invisible much of the time, yet always there, always available, the most reliable of the aides indicating

83

with a near-imperceptible nod of her head *I know my place: I am happy in my place* thus who would have suspected her of harboring a certain cruelty in her heart, Kathleen Hennessy's gaze veiled and retreating and her small smile only in response to others' inviting encouraging smiles thus who would have had cause to suspect her? and why? since the death that March morning though unexpected was not entirely unexpected, the patient was a woman of young middle age but exhausted from her ordeal, cerebrovascular disease with complications caused by diabetes, too weak to respond to visitors thus isolated in a private room amid a rich fantasy of potted flowers—mums, azalea, hydrangea—afterward it would be charged against the hospital that she should have been removed to intensive care for closer monitoring since her condition was proving so inert, slow to improve after surgery five days before and she'd run a fever of 101° F. from a hospital infection they'd finally managed to bring down to 99° F. but still she had to be fed by gavage, liquid formula funneled slowly and painstakingly through a feeding tube inserted in one of her nostrils and taped tight in place and according to the nurse who began the feeding procedure and the nurse's aide who completed it and remained afterward to tidy up there had been no apparent change in the woman's condition: respiration normal, heartbeat normal, response to the feeding normal, which is to say "normal" in that diminished context.

After all resuscitation efforts failed, and the floor doctor had no choice but to declare the patient dead, probable cause of death "cardiac arrest," already without needing to be told the nurse's aide Kathleen Hennessy had gone to fetch the death pack and was now deftly beginning to prepare the corpse for viewing by the family and eventually for the hospital morgue *I don't mind I don't mind I don't mind if I do: it's my job why should I mind?* but the nasty dried clot of semen was never entirely removed from her black pleated wool skirt from Hudson's.

Four

Sometimes Orson Abbott appeared to take no more notice of Kathleen Hennessy than if a column of airborne dust moved in her place, his frowning gaze piercing her, seeing nothing, registering nothing, so she shivered being so annihilated, erased *As if I had never been, as if he'd never touched me* but at other unexpected times as if drawn against the grain of his will and against even his sexual desire the young man discovered himself staring at her avidly, hungrily, his lips slightly raised from his teeth in a semblance of a smile and his glasses winking with a look of baffled rage. And this too she saw. All this she saw. Murmuring, "—Oh hello

Dr. Abbott—" her voice breathless and audacious and her shy-gliding past him so discreetly timed he need not acknowledge her at all if he so wished.

Always in the spring of 1972 it seemed *she* was there, at the shimmering periphery of his vision: that squat passive mammalian figure that, even clothed, appeared nude: the head modest, small, the face foreshortened and negligible as in one of those late Renoir nudes, boneless flesh: *she* bearing no apparent consciousness of herself, no sociable flirtatiousness or coquetry of the kind to which he was accustomed, had been accustomed since boyhood.

Yet never reproachful. Not a hint of bitterness.

And no irony in calling him, not Orson, but Dr. Abbott.

Not quite daring to smile at him, always hurrying past him on plump muscular legs, noiseless, a warm yeasty smell in her wake, all brisk hospital business. Cow. Cunt. Not you.

Yet it might have been that he dreamt of her. Grinding his teeth, writhing. That smothering mammalian flesh pressing close about him, balloon breasts filling his mouth, suffocation, horror, scratchy pubic hair chafing his chest . . . and he'd wake himself with a violent motion before the crisis of orgasm—Oh no, oh no no you *don't.*

What was his prescription for getting through his days, his nights, his thirty-six-hour shifts at the hospital, sunshine like broken glass on the John Lodge Expressway, vacant cement-sky impacted overhead?—one Quaalude behind two Dexedrine. The points of the fingers and the eyeballs electrically charged with that energy that could give life, or the semblance of life, to the dead.

These final months of Orson Abbott's medical career, twenty-eight years old, slipping down, failing, you can gauge the degree of your failure in the eyes of others calculating you, assessing you, which made him edgy defensive bad-tempered as he'd been as an intern at Columbia Presbyterian *Orson Abbott?—is he the son of?*—yes he was the son of, how could he not be the son of, Larry Abbott the internist, vascular surgeon, prominent in Michigan medical politics and pal of the Governor's and physician to the Grosse Pointe auto multimillionaires, yes he was the son of that father as no one ever allowed him to forget a fact which filled him with rage and guilt and anxiety and even childlike incredulity guessing that even so his medical career—his "future"—was rapidly running out. The speedy pills sharpened his hearing, his very eyesight, he could see around corners.

Not that he could not bear it otherwise, his life as a doctor. Not that he could not bear for instance the welfare cases, the flood of suffering and inarticulate humanity, malnourished and stunted and lice-ridden and frequently battered children, whites, blacks, Hispanics, West Indian, Asian, the startling "ethnic" population of a great American city until now obscured from his consciousness; not that he could not bear the surreal horror of the emergency room for instance, the vehicular accident victims with third- and even fourth-degree burns, slices missing from their heads, crushed arms and legs, snapped backbones, raw oozing abrasions like liquid flame, and the gunshot and stabbing victims of the city known as Murder City, U.S.A., most of them young black men, "black youths" in newspaper jargon bent on killing one another; not even that he could not bear the day upon day pathos of the elderly and the impoverished, the speechless terror of those paralyzed thus living-in-the-process-of-dying—but that he suspected, Orson Abbott the son of Larry Abbott, he could learn to bear it all very well, in time: to become professional: to move on, to move away, to take up a suburban practice too, to forget.

So: in this gradual downward skid that was at times perversely satisfying depending upon the oscillations of the drug/drugs monitoring Orson Abbott's tight-strung nervous system he had no time for her that nurse's aide whatever her name, so stricken with surprise or awe or calf-love she'd have let him fuck her in his car in the semidark without a word of acknowledgment let alone endearment or compassion—he had no time, he was revolted by her, ignored her yet there one humid evening in the hospital cafeteria when his head buzzed there he was pulling out a chair beside her, sitting, with no word of greeting observing how she continued to stir sugar into her already diluted coffee so he stopped her hand, "Easy: you're getting fat," and she winced, staring at him, her small recessed eyes that appeared just slightly crossed going suddenly liquid in hurt, in surrender.

Quickly she said, "Oh!—I'm sorry."

The spoon clattered onto the table, fell to the floor.

So often she winced, even whimpered.
When he touched her and his touch turned mean.

YA: Young Adult was the library code but Kathleen Hennessy was not the only adult woman who checked them from the Second Avenue branch of the Detroit Public Library *Nurse Lesley's Lost Love, Nurse Brenda's Challenge, Calling Nurse Abigail!, Nurse Rosemary Ames Reporting, Nurse Caroline and the Mystery at Avalon Manor, Nurse Barbara's Romance, Nurse Darlene's First Year, Nurse Lucy's Broken Heart, Judy Robinson—Registered Nurse, Lucy Jackson—Army Nurse, Kathy Cameron—Student Nurse* uniformly packaged two-hundred-page books with illustrated covers and dog-eared pages and print large enough not to cause eyestrain or psychic discomfort and though she read slowly sometimes with painstaking slowness moving her forefinger slow beneath each word as she sounded it silently in her head she was able to read one of these well within the two-week space allowed by the library, sometimes returning one and checking out another within so brief a space it seemed to her that the librarian smiled at her with approval as Mrs. Feinberg had once smiled at her *Now Kathleen of course you can do it: stop saying you can't!*

He said, "—Your head isn't peanut-sized actually, is it, up close. Just sometimes at a distance. How can that be explained? Optics?"

Myopic without his glasses, a dreamy wonder in his face.

There was Sally one of the nurse's aides on the floor, there was that young girl Trish just out of high school, and Midge Fleming who was Kathleen's special friend on the floor and they were all wearing engagement rings new since Christmas and Kathleen was very happy for them not at all envious or jealous for it seemed logical to her that God showered His gifts, say, upon a certain group of human beings as a flood of sunshine might move upon them thus if you were in the midst of the blessed His blessing might soon strike you too wasn't that logical?—wasn't that His way?—so Kathleen tried to choose her companions carefully at work and at the Fellowship (though all who belonged were Christians it did seem some were more happy in their faith than others, and certainly God's blessings fell more lavishly upon some than upon others) hoping that God would judge her kindly *O Lord see into my heart and make me whole* and in the hospital it was the young married women patients who most fascinated her, Kathleen always looked at once to see was a woman married, or engaged, was she wearing rings on her left hand *Why her and not me? why her and not me?* and always she smiled at them hoping they would smile at her in turn which some did, yes but others were preoccupied with worry or pain or they were drugged and incapable of noticing Kathleen Hennessy standing staring at their bedsides, not assigned to the OB ward she encountered patients of this age group less frequently thus a youngish woman or girl whether married or otherwise was something of a novelty in any case *She isn't any prettier than I am—is she?* and once she brought a meal tray to a young woman of her own age who wore a gold wedding band on her left hand and a gold engagement ring with a raised calyx of small diamonds that caught even the meager sunlight and turned it to flame, a young woman hospitalized for an emergency appendectomy and now recovering but frightened by her ordeal, shadows in her face, her fragile good looks smudged as if with a crude hand, Kathleen stood hesitantly smiling by her bed and the young woman said sharply, "Why are you looking at me like that?" and when Kathleen did not reply, too confused to reply, she said, her voice rising, "You—please— why are you looking at me like that? *I don't like it,*" so Kathleen stammered an apology and backed away and feared the young woman would complain to her doctor or the floor nurse or to her family but nothing came of it so far as Kathleen knew.

Most of all Kathleen Hennessy feared in this spring of 1972: false tales told of her to Orson Abbott or in Orson Abbott's hearing.

A sensation as of fiery red ants ran over her from the tips of her toes to the very scalp of her head, she shivered thinking *They better not, oh! they better not! Oh God You would not allow that would You!*

Tumescent, his penis grew stout as a rod, swelling to the point of pain yet not bursting: hardened as if calcified.

He laughed frightened as his body began rapidly to diminish—his legs, his arms, all his blood rushing into his penis leaving his brain oxygen-deprived, his senses askew, muscles small as a child's. And his ribs poking through his tight-drawn skin, his collar bone, how skinny he'd become, how sunken and glittery his eyes, he told her, "Suck me off for Christ's sake—*get busy,*" staring in loathsome fascination as she crouched over him wordless and immediate, her enormous breasts drooping, the enormous nipples, her belly a creased sack, a patch of pubic hair exactly the color and the texture of the hair on her head, her

low forehead abbreviated as she knelt clumsily on
the edge of the bed lowering her face to his penis
and he wasn't able to watch, whatever her name,
whoever, cow-cunt, her cunt was her mouth but
her mouth was maybe a cleaner cunt, he shut his
eyes laughing, he was a little boy whimpering,
half-sobbing, at the end he could not stop himself
from seizing her bobbing head in his hands her
hard head like a coconut that thick bushy crackly
hair in his frantic hands and he was out of control
his frantic hips and pelvis raised to her, thrusting
up into her as he gripped her head again, again,
again until he heard a scream rebound from the
walls of whatever room this was as Orson Abbott's
life shot foaming from him and into her: her:
whatever her name, whatever her face: who?

Five

He was not cruel but he was practical.

If not always practical, procedural.

He forbade her to wait for him in the hospital however inconspicuously or in any place close outside the hospital though the bus stop on Gratiot was allowable because it could be considered neutral territory: and she did after all take the bus: and if he happened to come by, if their schedules worked out that way, by accident, all right—"But look, Kathleen: I'm not promising anything."

She was not, however, to linger in those parts of the hospital in which he was on duty or through which he'd be likely to pass nor was she to approach him ever under any circumstances when he was in the company of others or in the cafeteria even if sitting by himself—"When I'm alone it's because I want to be alone." Granted, he could hardly forbid her to *see* him if the encounter was by chance but he'd be very upset yes and very angry if she stared at him in that way of hers every emotion showing on her face like an infant's, so painfully obvious.

He said, "It's for your own good, Kathleen: I wouldn't want you to be hurt."

She nodded. She understood. Giving Orson Abbott a swift shy sidelong glance even as (in one instance, in Abbott's car as he drove making his way through a maze of one-way streets somewhere to the south of Detroit Metropolitan Hospital in the hazy dusk of summer twilight) driving with his habitual air of distraction as if forgetful of the fact that he was driving a car at all and that, behind the wheel, he had an obligation not to drift into the lanes of other cars, or press down on the gas pedal so erratically, his glasses sliding down his nose so he had to push them back up repeatedly, amphetamine heat lifting from his pale skin with a smell as of a child's fever) he cast a sidelong glance at her, strangely shy as well, perplexed.

"D'you understand?—I wouldn't want you to be hurt."

Excitedly she worried she might be pregnant for her period did not come, and did not come, and her belly seemed puffy, yes and her breasts more sensitive than usual even as she knew she could not be pregnant—*could she? oh!*—for Orson Abbott in his fastidiousness had not made love to her in quite that way, keeping himself from her fully it sometimes seemed as if fearful of her or in dread of her sometimes hardly speaking to her during their time together and if her love for him shone in her face he shielded his eyes from it or made one of his dry droll shrugging jokes saying goodbye so she dared not speak either except with her eyes *I love love love you Orson I would die for you, tell me anything I might do and I will do it* and then in the midst of a minor emergency on the floor, a newly admitted patient shouting and struggling with one of the male orderlies, she felt the first seeping of blood in her loins so she was not pregnant after all.

God's will be done.

In Your own time.

She dreamt: God had ordained she was an angel of the sick and the dying: she was a Catholic nun wearing a dazzling-white habit, floor-length skirts and wimple, and high starched cap so impractical but lovely, and her beads of prayer worn at her belt, swaying and clicking like half-heard music as she moved swiftly noiselessly from bed to bed bringing God's mercy to the infirm.

She dreamt: there was a ring on the third finger of her left hand!—a luminous jewel, like the very crystal-beads of her rosary arranged in a calyx so glowing bright she could scarcely look at it *oh! more real than anything real* so when she woke confused she sat up staring and blinking at her hand, her ringless hand, that pudgy hand with the short-filed nails, yes and her other hand was ringless too for of course jewelry was forbidden at the hospital most of the time and she had no true jewelry anyway, only cheap things that left tarnish stains on her skin, she was crying silently the ring in her dream had after all been so real, so remarkably real *oh so much more real* than anything she knew.

He said, "It's weird isn't it—everybody wanting to live. You see it in others, the desperation, the terror, it's so self-evidently comical, all these people, too many people"—waving his hand in an extravagant careless gesture as he drove, northbound on Gratiot, "—but in yourself, either you can't see it, or won't."

And he began to laugh. That laugh of his so boyish baring his perfect straight teeth showing the glisten of saliva on his lips, a contagious sort of laugh so Kathleen laughed too, for very joy.

In church silently she gave thanks praying behind her hands pressed to her face, what she did was sin even if she did not so much do it as allow it to be done, rejoice in its being done *Oh! again again again* and opening her eyes wide and startled seeing, yes she was in church still, the congregation of strangers in the pews about her, the new minister at the pulpit (for Reverend Deck who'd liked Kathleen so much had left Detroit for a ministry elsewhere) preaching with a forefinger raised in warning, his sombre face above his white collar reminding her nonetheless of one of those little fruit pies with a fluted wrapper, you bought the little pie and ate it out of your hand in the corner store, and her mouth flooded with saliva that was yet a kind of gratitude for very life, for such senses as taste and smell and eyesight and hearing *O Lord*

God thank You: from whom all blessings flow her
adoration shining in her eyes so the minister Reverend Peppler kept glancing at her as if distracted.

The other nurse's aides knew of Orson Abbott's
love for Kathleen Hennessy and were jealous. Following her with their eyes. Smiling behind their
fingers.

And Midge: Midge she'd have sworn was her
true friend: cornering her in the nurses' lounge
saying she'd been hearing some things about Kathleen that sort of worried her, one of the residents
was it? one of those hot-shit young doctors?—
just remember to be careful Midge said meaning
CAREFUL—, and Kathleen turned upon her a
face of such contorted fury the woman stepped
backward as if she'd been slapped and afterward
told the others she couldn't have been more shocked
if the ceiling had caved in or there'd been an earth-
quake—"My God can you imagine? Kathleen of
all people? Looking at me like she wanted to kill
me?" so Kathleen began to think then she might
have to leave the hospital where she'd been so
happy but there were always positions open for
nurse's aides with experience and it would not matter to Orson Abbott where she worked in fact he
might be relieved if she worked at another hospital

or clinic so they could see each other without fear of gossip and in any case maybe she'd be married soon, married soon and pregnant with her first baby *and never have to work again: that will show them* but she'd cried just the same, these many months she'd thought those women were all her friends.

Thursdays her shift ended at 8 p.m. but at 11 p.m. there she was huddled out of the rain in the graffiti-scrawled bus shelter and one of his companions nudged him and he saw her and stood for a long moment wordless staring at her letting the rain soak his hair and his clothes then the others went on and he came to her, she flinched a little seeing his face but his hands on her were gentle, gently he framed her face with his fingers staring at her as if he'd never truly seen her before stretching the skin back tight from her eyes, "—oh Christ how long have you been waiting here," his mouth beginning to twitch like a child's, "—I know you: the one who gives everything and gets nothing in return: 'the insulted and injured' and forgive me I'm doing it to you too, I don't mean to Kathleen but I'm doing it to you too—" and his voice trailed off bewildered and aggrieved and seeing that he did not seem angry or humiliated by her in his companions' presence Kathleen slipped her arms around him and lay her cheek against his chest, how tall he was *oh! how tall! his arms encircling me his beloved Kathleen* and in a mutual swoon they stood there for a long long time.

Drinks at a tavern on Cass where no one was likely to recognize them, sometimes he'd pick up a few dollars' worth of reputedly high-quality hashish which Kathleen demurred from smoking: just didn't want to, she said: maybe fearing her nurse superiors would be able to detect it on her breath in the morning, or might her eyes be dilated or the pupils pinpricks so he laughed at her, but didn't force her, it was a time when his hands on her didn't force her, nor his knees nudging her knees apart, nor his penis nudging against her as if groping blind seeking entry and entering though almost immediately his thin pale body would shudder and sweat break out at every pore as he came, and came, helplessly, whimpering like a frightened child into the plump creases of her neck, sobbing *Oh oh oh oh oh.*

So that then Kathleen in a transport of bliss might hold him in her arms, hold him precious inside her tensing her vaginal muscles to keep him for as long as she could until the shrinking rubbery little thing slipped from her and Orson Abbott slept exhausted his mouth slack and one of his arms dangling limp over the side of the bed *as you must never allow any patient to remain: never an arm or a leg dangling, never a head lolling oh never* and after a time Kathleen slept too but only lightly as if skimming the surface of sleep slantwise not daring to plunge deeply, to fall.

Or: walking in urban light refracted as aquarium glass, their arms around each other's waist he'd say quietly, "—You should think about your future, Kathleen," just perceptibly to her ear an air of strain as he pronounced her name: "Kathleen": as if its taste were exotic on his tongue, saying, "—You should find a better job, for one thing. Stop letting them exploit you. Colonize you. The hospital is a business, a capitalist enterprise, they're out for profits and they treat nurses like shit let alone nurse's aides and orderlies, janitors, secretaries, anyone they can get away with treating like shit including in fact the young professionals meaning me but there's some point to my enslavement even though I'm about to be thrown out on my ass," beginning to laugh, or was he coughing, Orson Abbott had been a horrified witness earlier that night to an operating table death, sudden hemorrhaging as if a balloon had been pricked and the patient had gone into instantaneous shock and died within minutes despite the most strenuous efforts to save him but Orson Abbott was not going to think of that now shivering, tightening his arm around this short squat young woman's waist, "—anyway never mind me, it's you, you're the subject: what about you?"

Kathleen murmured something vague and near-inaudible.

Orson said, "Huh? What's that?"

Kathleen said hesitantly, "I—guess I don't feel that way. I—"

"Don't feel what way?"

"Oh—that the hospital treats me like—"

"Like shit?"

"Oh—" her intake of breath was forcible, "—but I don't feel that way Orson, I love my job, I—I'm proud of my job."

She spoke not stubbornly, nor yet flirtatiously, but with a simple adamant conviction.

And Orson Abbott laughed again, and sighed, no derision in him now but melancholy resignation, looking at this young woman with the color in her cheeks, small shining eyes, laboring for an hourly wage fifteen cents above the minimum hourly wage set by the Congress of the United States some years before and inadequate then: so always the exploited, the underclass of imperialist America, thousands of poorly educated young men shipped off like cattle to die in an insane "war" in Vietnam that privileged young men like Orson Abbott might not only be spared but spared for the continuation of their self-advancement; so always the pure of heart, the unquestioning, the meek and the lame and the halt and the blind and they that hunger after righteousness and shall inherit not the Earth but mere dirt shoveled into their mouths.

Orson said roughly, "Of course. You should be proud. You're a damned good nurse's aide."

Later that night adding, "Still: you could go to nursing school, couldn't you. Upgrade yourself a little."

She smiled confused, frightened, beginning to shake her head as a dog might shake its head, "Oh—oh no, I—I wouldn't be smart enough for nursing school"—her voice fading on a note of appeal—"Would I?"

He asked her what was her life and she seemed utterly baffled by the question: Life?

In the two-room apartment in the paint-peeling woodframe house on Second Avenue, a row of elm stumps at the curb, atop her bedroom bureau a doily and atop that neatly arranged in a triangular figure a rosary of cheap plastic beads coiled like a small snake, a retouched sentimental photograph of the late President John F. Kennedy, in an identical dimestore-gilt frame a likeness of Jesus Christ on the cross seen close up, blood droplets from the crown of thorns on His forehead, soulful Italian eyes heavy-lidded as in an erotic slumber—"I didn't know you were Catholic: are you?"

No she wasn't Catholic, seemed embarrassed to be asked.

Saying after a moment that she went sometimes to the United Methodist Church on Woodward, Sunday services at 9 a.m., yes she believed in God she told him solemnly, and in Jesus Christ His only son—"There is no other way."

"No other way—?"

"No. *No.*"

He asked did her family live in Detroit, it was the first time in their months of knowing each other he'd ever asked her any questions of a personal nature thus the color deepened in her cheeks, she was shy-stammering but in bliss at being so questioned, his hands gentle on her, on the edge of impatience but gentle, no her family didn't live in

Detroit she said hesitantly, they lived up north she said, a long pause as if she meant to continue but did not so he asked, genuinely curious, "Where 'up north' exactly?" and she laughed nervously, said, lifting her small pudgey hands, the nails so carefully filed and buffed, unpolished, "—Oh the North Pole!" giggling as if she were being tickled then falling silent and in the aftermath of this, Kathleen Hennessy's first attempt at humor in Orson Abbott's presence, Orson Abbott did not pursue the subject.

Kneeling awkwardly before her his arms slung around her hips, face mashed against her belly, her warm yeasty-smelling crotch, squeezing and squeezing her as if he meant to determine with his own bones the fact of hers so secret and impacted in her flesh as outside on Second Avenue traffic streamed past with a sound of bemused impatience and bars of radiant plaited light leapt skidding onto the walls of the shabby little bedroom smelling of talcum powder and that harsh germicide solution the hospital issued for handwashing, he was murmuring words he could not himself quite hear, *Love love love oh God, oh God* in a delirium of desire as she winced at his embrace yet unprotesting acquiesced to it, always she whoever she was, this one, this short dumpy big-breasted one, sweet-faced one, baby cow, silky cunt, always she acquiesced, *Oh God: God* he squeezed as if intending now to squeeze the very life out of her who so violently sucked his life from him, she swayed above him staggering, whimpering, yet still unprotesting for if he dug his nails into her as he'd done upon more than one occasion, yes digging his nails into her very cunt she would not protest and he was speedy now from Dexedrine he'd taken a long time ago but it seemed to be reviving in him, flashing and melting along his nerves, that hard hot angry rod between his legs and he was hallucinating in flashes the two of them on the floor now and he was tearing at her clothing, lifting her skirt, the white-nylon fabric, tearing her underwear, hallucinating as if from a short distance as if was it a classroom? one of those lecture halls with graduated seats rising from a platform at the front, a podium and blackboard? yes and a laboratory sink? at U-M where he'd done his undergraduate work too preparing singlemindedly through the semesters for medical school in the prestigious school in which Larry Abbott had distinguished himself and there came the précis "The Rise of Life on Earth" seemingly both idea and actual glimpsed phenomena-flood as the chemical yielded mysteriously to the biological, Earth acquiring life, heat, volition, a central nervous system, out of primary water-ammonia-hydrogen-methane arose organic compounds of amino acids, mononucleotides, sugars, how then did these evolve into the long polymer chains required for life, how then when such forms are known to be unstable and vulnerable to solar ultraviolet rays and to water yet the chains did evolve, millions upon millions of years and how then did such inanimate material self-reproduce, replicate, what then is the principle of the organic, why then evolution shifting from the chemical to the biological, what destiny?—*N.B.: amino acids used in living forms are exclusively left-handed, all sugars so used are right-handed* why? don't ask nor ask why the emergence of life-forms out of such mere matter and the evolution of these life-forms into ever more complex labyrinthine structures of flesh, bone, nerve simply to replicate DNA strands? he was beginning to laugh, his penis so grotesquely swollen like a club, the genital sensation so powerful as to be near-annihilating yet still he was scribbling in his notebook sweating there in his creaking seat in the lecture hall *N.B.: why 'junk' nucleotides in DNA? to what purpose???* giggling he resolved to ask at some future date, millions of years would pass, unfathomable brain-quenching millions like the LSD-years of intergalactic space in *2001* like the Earth-measured miles between this planet and Tau Ceti, out of the brainless gas-liquid-solid of the biosphere how then primitive protozoa how then vertebrates how then brain stems how then *Homo sapiens* at last upright with speech don't ask, the cerebellum, the cerebral cortex, *I I I* thrusting to what purpose don't ask, he was kneading this pliant female flesh like bread dough, he was slamming himself into her so deep into her her ass had begun to skid by slow half-inches across the splintery floorboards of whichever room this was and he held pried far apart the fattish knees with his own bony knees, this female lying flat and helpless on an examining table her legs spread, bare feet in metal stirrups so she couldn't flinch to escape so achingly pitilessly exposed her vagina like raw red flesh lacking an epidermis like something incompletely born expelled from the uterus and there the pubic hair a patch of coarse animal fur, he was coming, he was trying to come, his heart pounding choking in his chest in his throat, sweat in rivulets stinging his face, his sides, even his skinny thighs but the more violently he thrust himself into her the harder his erection became, a rod a club seemingly permanent and unyielding no tenderness could dissolve it until she began whimpering louder, pleading at last at last not words but sheer sound rising from her frightened throat rising to a scream still he was trying to come and could not and then she screamed. And then he came.

Six

And then, she was assisting in a surgical
scrub, she was at the scrub sink, she
required to be sterile required to scrub:
the 10-minute scrub, timed to assist
others scrubbing, surgeon, assistants, scrub nurse,
nurse's aides Mute, a white cap tight covering her hair *All persons understood to
be contaminated, all surfaces not sterile
are contaminated.* Counting days, she had
not seen him (in fact she had: had seen: at a distance: he had not known) nor heard
She was not crying, she was mute performing at the scrub sink, her first surgical

scrub but brisk unhesitating   unblinking
following   instructions   aseptic technique,
open   outer wrapper of   (2 brushes & 2
files)   (2 towels)   (glove package)
Transient bacteria on the skin's   surface, resident bacteria under the fingernails (subungual)
and in the deeper layers   of the skin   in hair
follicles in openings of sebaceous glands   however after minutes scrubbing BACTERIA   in
deeper layers   are BROUGHT TO THE
SURFACE OF THE SKIN   and the bac-
terial count on the previously scrubbed   skin
is again very high   for this reason sterile gloves
Periodic cultures taken from the hands   and
arms of   hospital personnel Counting days:
weeks: sticking a finger deep to hurt,   checking for   blood but   she was not crying, now
was she laughing   At the scrub sink
wrapped in white, a cap tight covering her hair
as the others talked   she could feel it inside her
now it was thirty-five days,   a glowing gem

Pick up brush touching only the back not the
bristles,   apply several drops of detergent:
begin timing   scrub in a pattern   begin at
thumb, then each finger   palm of hand   back

of hand and arm   scrub each hand and arm
with brush No. 1   for 2 minutes : timed
then discard brush   rinse hands and arms
alowing water to run down from fingertips to
elbows   do not shake water droplets off
Pick up file cleaning subungual spaces under
running   Discard file   Pick up second brush,
repeat scrub   with brush No. 2 for 3 minutes :
timed   After rinsing keep hands and arms up
away from body   Pick up folded sterile towel
at arm's length   Allow to unfold   place one
end over one hand   dry the other hand and arm
in a blotting rotation motion   working from
hand to elbow do not retrace any area   Powder
hands   from sterile peel-back packet
Discard packet into receptacle   Pinch up flap
of envelope containing right glove   with the
right hand, grasp glove by folded edge of
remove gauze inserts   discard   Grasping
turned-down cuff pull the glove over the hand
adjust fingers of gloves to insure fit over fingertips

Surgical debridement involves the excision of all
contaminated and dead tissue leaving the wound
enlarged with clean live tissue with freshly
trimmed edges   that can be apposed for closure

The surgeon distinguishes live tissue from dead
live tissue is moist pink and firm to touch
muscle will contract   free bleeding from cut
capillary vessels   Dead tissue is dark and
infirm does not bleed

Seven

Pregnant forty days, forty-one days, she knew
the signs and was not frightened, she had no fear
in her, though waiting sometimes in the bus stop
shelter late at night she guessed it might be dan-
gerous, the winos, the rummies, heroin users nod-
ding off, and the smell of urine she scarcely noticed
and the gaseous clouds of poison from the rears
of the Detroit city buses stopping and pulling away
and stopping and pulling away but Kathleen Hennessy did not notice, if others saw her she did not
see them, if they whispered of her smiling behind
their hands shaking their heads in pity she did
not see, she was thinking of her lover, she was

thinking of not why would he not see her now nor
even acknowledge her she would not have asked
even for a smile, she was not thinking of such matters standing calm and flat-footed a mature woman
by the look of her, a full figure, full pie-shaped
face ruddy with health, the rosiness of pregnancy
and did they know? the others on the floor? did
her superiors know? the other tenants in her house?
but she was not thinking of such things in fact she
was thinking of when would it happen: when
would Orson Abbott appear and what signs might
accompany his appearance *Counting the city buses*
or *the out-of-state license plates* or in the pocket
of her coat Betty Lou's rosary she was in the habit
of bringing with her to the hospital now *I didn't
know you were Catholic: are you?*

He said, "Jesus. You shouldn't cry. It changes
your face to a pig's—a pig's snout." He laughed,
he ran both hands through his spiky sweaty hair,
he was in his hospital whites gaunt and fearful of
her, "—I'm serious: people with faces like yours
should not cry except in private," his laughter
thinly rising and the pupils of his eyes contracted
to pinpricks, Kathleen was not crying now and
then he rushed her striking her with his balled
fists, "Pig! pig! disgusting pig!" forcing her back

against the wall as she tried to shield both her face and her belly and he raised his knee panting, he was furious, half-sobbing as she'd never seen him, the heat flying off him, "You did it on purpose didn't you! on purpose didn't you! Pig!" but afterward lying sobbing on the bed he allowed her to cradle his head in her lap, she pressed a cloth soaked in cold water against his burning forehead and he told her how sorry, oh God how sorry, he wasn't like that at all really he was not an exploiter of women or of anyone truly he didn't know what came over him it was the Dexedrine it was those sons of bitches at the hospital it was his father out in Grosse Pointe with his million-dollar practice it was the unspeakable war in Vietnam shaming all who lived at this time a wound festering and gangrenous never now to be made well so Kathleen Hennessy saw that it was not she whom Orson Abbott loathed nor yet their baby-to-be but these other factors thus *I will wait: I can wait* cradling her fiancé's head thinking of Jesus Christ on His cross believing even His Father had forsaken Him, all He was willing to endure knowing it was so written.

The thing is Kathleen we must never never lose faith in ourselves for faith is everything though she

could not now remember who had told her that,
nor why.

Yet also: *Better to learn now than later* but she
could not remember who had told her that either
except it was a long time ago.

Thus soft-spoken but resolute Kathleen Hennessy informed her superiors she would be quitting
her job as of January first, she had a new job she
told them closer to where her family lived "on the
east side," her mouth twitched once or twice but
she did not cry but almost she did cry when Midge
hugged her so hard saying she'd miss her, they'd
all miss her—but afterward it wasn't the same now
they all knew she was leaving, hearing her friends
talking and laughing together then they'd go quiet
as she approached so she worried did they know
about her secret swelling deep inside her belly,
the ache of her breasts her rocky sensation morn-
ings though not once had she vomited *Nature pre-
pares both mother and baby physiologically for
this great event: pregnancy is not a 'pathological
condition'!* thus how could they know? even nurses,
how could they know? These weeks she'd been
wearing a girdle to minimize the puffiness of her
belly and her white uniform was a little tight but

120

as often as she could she wore a white cotton smock over it thus how could they know?

No longer now did she think in misery *Doesn't he love me, does he want it dead* because she knew.

No longer now did she think her fingers twisted in secret about her rosary *If I count ten out-of-state license plates* because she knew.

And no longer the surprise and embarrassment of sudden tears as that time just before Thanksgiving on the Second Avenue bus 6:05 a.m. *I want to have my baby, it's my baby, I would not then ever be lonely again* her face contorted in an instant and raw sobs issuing from her so her face was a pig's she knew but could not stop crying, others on the bus staring at her until a heavyset Negro lady leaned over to ask Honey you all right? Hey honey? and Kathleen managed to explain to the Negro lady that her mother had died only the day before and she got off the bus at the next stop no matter she had a mile to walk to the hospital but that would never happen again because she knew. *Better to learn now than later.*

Nurse's aides with experience were wanted to work in hospitals, nursing homes, private residences in Detroit and suburbs, each Sunday the newspaper carried help wanted advertisements so

Kathleen was given to believe she would not have trouble finding a job. Once she was ready.

She had saved up some money. She would not ask him for money. She was going to be all right.

It gave her satisfaction to recall that always in her life she had been all right.

Now that she knew: she knew there was no hope: knowing there is no hope can be a wonderful thing and now she knew, now she would do it, what must be done, for Kathleen Hennessy's nature was practical and procedural after all. Not romantic, nor deluded. Sobriety best suited her. Brushes and detergent. Diagrams. White nylon, white stockings, and white rubber-soled shoes.

Frowning over *Handbook* diagrams of pregnancy: the mother's body; the baby and the intra-uterine structures; the baby and the birth canal; first, second, and third stages of labor; the delivery of the baby; the delivery of the placenta. Two hundred eighty days was the approximate full term of pregnancy but she would abort the fetus before it acquired eyes, a mouth, a voice, a soul thus there could be no sin; or, if sin, she would never think of it as such for that was not Kathleen Hennessy's nature as leaving the hospital after their shifts all but the newest and youngest of hospital workers stopped thinking of what they had witnessed or participated in that day not out of callousness or indifference but sheer expediency. So practical was Kathleen's nature that by November and December of 1972 she did not even think it remarkable that a young man of Orson Abbott's presumed intelligence, a University of Michigan Medical School graduate in residency at Detroit Metropolitan Hospital who knew that he had impregnated her seemed to have forgotten the fact as one might forget any trivial fact, an evening or an hour's diversion that failed to meet expectations thus might simply be erased from memory: for now again Kathleen had ceased to exist for him, at first he conspicuously avoided her upon one occasion passing her on the stairs outside the cafeteria his eyes fixedly averted and his lips pursed in whistling a thin jaunty nervous tune while she froze shrinking her small eyes shrinking smaller but subsequent times Orson Abbott appeared truly oblivious of her especially in the company of his fellows who chancing to see her—not her: a nurse or a nurse's aide, without identity—looked through her as if she were no more than airborne dust and Kathleen acquiesced to the logic of it, and even the justice *Treats people like you like shit: pig-face, pig-snout* turning away her dignity shrinking but intact.

Except: those final days at the hospital not in stealth yet unobtrusively and wholly without detection (for who would suspect her) Kathleen methodically prepared for what she thought of simply as *It;* and unobtrusively and wholly without detection, almost without awareness, she saturated several small sponges with the mouth-suction drainage of a hepatitis patient (a black man in his twenties, a heroin user, six feet tall and wasted to one hundred pounds) to carry into the private and semiprivate rooms on the floor and to introduce to patients as opportunity granted in drinking water, in foods, on linens, in mouthwash and toothpaste: and whether hepatitis spread through this part of the hospital, with more virulence than the usual hospital infection, or whether little came of it, Kathleen would not know. She rarely read the newspapers, even to scan the headlines. She would have other more urgent matters on her mind in the days to follow.

Eight

A knife handle No. 3 with a No. 15 blade taken from a minor surgery kit; a scrub package; a glove package; one dozen thick absorbent cotton pads and a box of tampons; five Darvon tablets. And germicide-detergent solution.

First she showered. Washed her hair briskly, roughly with medicated shampoo.

Shaved her underarms and her legs which she had not shaved for some time. Then stooped awkwardly over the toilet—awkwardly because of her heavy belly—she shaved her pubic region methodically taking care not to cut herself; and flushed away the shavings. Then she covered her hair with a tight-fitting white cotton cap. Then still naked she returned to the bathtub where at first standing and then squatting on her heels she observed the procedural rules of the surgical scrub timing herself by counting aloud "One two three four" first scrubbing her hands and arms with germicide-detergent solution as she'd been trained then her torso, her legs, her feet and lastly her pubic region observing the procedural scrub rules which apparently she had memorized with no consciousness of having memorized them.

She had locked the door to her windowless bathroom. She had locked and bolted the door of her apartment.

In the other room she had turned the radio to a popular Detroit music station, the volume moderately high. She had timed the abortion for mid-morning of a January weekday when the other residents of her apartment house would all be at work thus should she weaken and scream no one would hear her even should her screams be audible over the radio or distinguishable from it.

She opened the sterile package containing the gloves and put the gloves on, left hand, right hand. She noted that her hands were beginning to tremble a little but to tremble evenly.

Squatting naked on her heels in the tub she held

a small mirror beneath her vagina and opened the labial lips wide to examine herself. She had sterilized the mirror by boiling it for thirty minutes in a pan on the stove, then carried it to the bathroom in the pan.

In the sink, in another pan, were a dozen ice cubes.

She had taken a Darvon tablet some minutes before.

She had begun to sweat at her hairline.

She examined her vaginal area for some time calculating how she would proceed. Essentially she had to transmogrify the familiar *Handbook* diagrams seen from the side into a diagram in her head seen from both below (for the surgical penetration would come from below) and above (for her consciousness, her hands came from above) and there was the further complication that the womb, the fetus, the intrauterine structure, were not visible in any way from any angle of vision external to the body.

How opaque, then, flesh. So solid so sturdy there as Kathleen Hennessy squatted on her heels in the narrow stained bathtub she'd scoured with germicide hearing a percussive beat issuing from the radio in the other room a mimicry of copulation's beat and beyond that on Second Avenue the sound of traffic passing like an erratic heartbeat *Whatever is, is now* thus she did not pray to God for His help.

The fetus was fourteen weeks old.

Yes she had felt it move inside her. Miniature tentative kicks. Yet the eyes were unopened.

Trying not to gag she placed one of the thick cotton pads in her mouth; gripped it with her teeth, her strong jaws.

She picked up the No. 3 knife handle with the No. 15 blade inserted into it flexing her fingers to become accustomed to the snug-fitting gloves. Made of a material so thin as to be nearly transparent, the material of condoms and susceptible to tears, breakage, thus the hands inside must be sterile at all times. The gravest danger was from infection of the birth canal unless the gravest danger was from hemorrhaging but of that she would not think counting "One two three four" waiting until the trembling in her hand subsided then spreading the vaginal lips she brought the razor-sharp blade upright against the cervix and into the birth canal even as she pressed down upon it grunting with surprise at the lightning-swift pain as if she had been thinking that the tiny creature in her uterus would feel it and not she. And immediately too a rivulet and then a stream of bright warm blood began to flow wetting her legs, her feet, her tense spread toes and she heard someone cry in astonishment *Oh! oh oh* muffled by the pad in her mouth.

Yet she judged that the insertion had not been deep enough, thus bringing the bloodied shiny instrument up inside herself a second time, a second time bearing down with all the weight of her sturdy body, grunting, gritting the pad between her teeth trying not to gag as a wave of violent nausea washed over her, and there was a flash of pain, and another, plaited radiant pain like bars of sunlight thrown across the wall, *Oh!* she nearly dropped the knife so slippery in her gloved fingers as now blood flowed swift as urine from between her legs as she maintained her clumsy posture swaying on her heels panting like an animal not desperate but resigned *Oh oh oh!* and a third time she bore the knife up inside her, now jamming it half-angrily into her and dropping it in nearly the same motion as her insides suddenly loosened, gushed hotly out between her legs *Oh oh oh* screaming inside the cotton pad then she was falling sideways, fainting, fighting for consciousness reviving not knowing whether she'd fainted but she'd fallen clumsily sideways in the tub, the knife under her thigh so she'd cut herself there too but there was no pain and not much bleeding, Kathleen was grinning her teeth clamped down hard on whatever it was in her mouth soaked in saliva, her body heaved with pain like a bell clapper inside a bell, blood running down the drain of the tub as she'd planned but the sight of it confused her and she was shivering violently so naked but sweating too and the panicked thought came to her that she should not be sweating after the scrub, fresh bacteria were being flushed to the surface of her skin and she was helpless to prevent the contamination. Darker strands of blood began to appear inside her bleeding, now bits of tissue, cupping her gloved hands under her between her legs she saw suddenly the tender skinless thing, the tiny fetus about the size of her palm, part of it jelly, part liquid running seeping through her fingers *Oh*   *oh oh.*

All persons understood to be contaminated, all surfaces not sterile are contaminated thus the day before she'd sterilized water by boiling it on the kitchen stove, sterilized the two ice cube trays from the freezing compartment of her refrigerator boiling them for thirty minutes and not a minute less now she pressed ice cubes against her vagina, numbing cold amid the blood, the strangeness of it, bleeding onto ice cubes yet there was a logic and Kathleen was beginning to feel elated despite the pain and shivering, she spat out the cotton pad soaked with saliva now she took up one of the thick white sanitary pads and held it between her legs with her trembling fingers until the blood soaked through, quickly the blood soaked through so she discarded it over the edge of the tub and opened another out of its wrapper and held it between her legs, in a few minutes a third, each thick pad soaked through and discarded and she had no idea how much time had passed it seemed that no time at all had passed and then cautiously she climbed out of the tub awkwardly holding a pad between her legs, the sight of the blood-splattered tub so distressed her she took time to turn on the shower to rinse it at least superficially then swallowed a second Darvon tablet and it seemed the painkiller had an immediate effect since she felt a floating sensation going into the adjoining room where the air was so much cooler and a radio voice greeted her affable and familiar and she went to her bed which she'd prepared, a rubber covering, several thicknesses of towels and she sat down carefully on the edge of the bed holding the sanitary pad in place then swung her legs which were oddly light onto the bed then lay back floating and smiling and she slept: waking hours later unable to recall at first what had happened, where she was, then feeling the cramps indistinguishable from menstrual cramps, feeling the surge of blood inside her loins and the pain now at a curious distance clearly hers, yet at a distance, so she lay very still understanding how in the human world she was invisible and would forever be thus and so her pain if it was pain and her suffering if it was suffering and the death of the tiny skinless thing meant to be her baby if it was a true death did not matter in the human world in the slightest *You're shit: pig's snout* and seemed not to matter much in God's world and she wondered if there were others of her kind and if these others knew of one another and knew of one another's secret strength, the terrible secret strength of those whom the human world has made invisible but it was the euphoria of the drug that granted Kathleen Hennessy such wisdom and perhaps she would not remember afterward or if she remembered she might think that someone had told her *You're shit: pig's snout* and not that it was her own soul which had spoken.

She had bled severely but she had not hemorrhaged. She would be all right. She did not doubt that she would be all right. When she was recovered she would begin work as a nurse's aide at the Twin Oaks Convalescent Home in the suburb of Hamtramck and soon there she would acquire a reputation for diligence for uncomplaining tractability for absolute reliability and no one was to suspect her of willful harm nor even of accidental harm in the care of patients to whom she was assigned if, say, a random death occurred now and then and no death in such a context is wholly unexpected but when it seemed to her that others were watching her closely she would quit and acquire another job as a nurse's aide this time at the Helene P. Olden Foundation Clinic in Livonia, two years later at the St. Francis of Assisi Rehabilitation Center in Detroit on West Outer Drive, she would work at other clinics and hospitals and private residences as the years passed and the years would pass swiftly as in a dream not her own as water yields unresisting to water *Now the worst has been done, now there is nothing* sometimes so pitying one of her helpless charges she would find herself pressing a pillow against the face, sometimes it was an indefinable and abruptly overpowering rage that moved her, the stuporous sleep of the drugged shading into the obdurate stillness and rigor of death *Now there is nothing again, again* and again she would prepare the body for the morgue as she'd been trained by this time having forgotten virtually all that preceded her life until that moment of serenity except to understand that, yes it had been done to her too, such deaths leave no marks, simply a cessation of life: which means Death: whatever it was that had been done had been done and Kathleen Hennessy was all right and would always be all right invisible thus excluded from the human world of power and authority and responsibility thus she was valued as the most trusted of workers, the most reliable, so unquestioning, so nearly mute she would prepare the bodies of countless strangers for countless morgues in a succession of robot-selves working just above the minimum wage performing by rote with unswerving confidence and always with secret satisfaction certain procedural rites pertaining to the dead and on this sun-swept January morning in Detroit, Michigan, in her shabby bedroom overlooking Second Avenue she lay quietly feeling the hot blood seep in her loins, the price of her freedom she didn't contest, her reddened eyes dilated she was breathing almost normally except occasionally when a needle of excruciating pain penetrated the Darvon haze and she moaned aloud without seeming to hear herself but she was going to be all right *Now the worst is done, now* of that

Kathleen Hennessy did not doubt. On her bedside table within easy reach was the sparkling crystal-bead rosary someone had given her years ago coiled neatly as always with the little stainless steel crucifix right-side up and visible as always. Also, a pitcher of water and a glass; the three remaining Darvon tablets laid out on a tissue; several sanitary pads; several chocolate candy bars; and *Nurse Eileen Goes to Alaska* its illustrated cover protected by a transparent plastic wrapper.